MW01181985

THE TIMELESS ZODIAC

Book I

The Timeless Zodiac
Book I

Written by

Dana Skvarek II

Cover and Illustrations by

Jolene Skvarek

Edited by

Jeff Goeson

2018

Copyright © 2017 by Vivifica Studios, LLC

All rights reserved. This book or any portion thereof may not be repro-
duced or used in any manner whatsoever without the express written per-
mission of the publisher except for the use of brief quotations in a book
review or scholarly journal.

First Printing 2017

Second Edition: 2018

ISBN 978-1-387-82969-9

Vivifica Studios, LLC
4381 North 75th St, Suite 201
Scottsdale, AZ 85251

www.VivificaStudios.com

Dedication

To those that have fought the Chaos in ages past, and to those
that must fight in ages to come.
Believe.

Chapter 1

"I have a story to tell," said the man with bull horns on his head. His ancient but fair eyes gazed across the battlefield, as he took in the destruction and horrors of war before him. To his left stood another man, far younger at thirty five years than the he, who's age was quite literally, timeless.

"This...is Paris?" asked the second man to the first.

"Was. Was Paris," the horned man replied in his deep resounding voice.

"I never thought I'd see it like this."

"No one ever does. Before I tell you the rest, you must believe me. There is no time to waste."

The horn-headed man stepped down from the rubble that hours ago was a bakery on the outskirts of downtown Paris, France. Without looking where hes going, he stomped on bricks and baguettes alike, all the while the other man stared out over the city.

"Taurus..." he asked, "can this be stopped?"

The larger man, Taurus the Bull, the Zodiac, the Time-less, an eternal, immortal being whose human-like eyes had witnessed the birth of the very galaxy he now shepherded, stopped short of crushing a burnt and broken mobile phone beneath his feet. As he looked back at the smaller man he noticed just how frail the human body really was.

"It can," he assured his tiny companion.

"But...you said it never has."

"This would be a first, yes."

The younger man continued to stare out at the city that once was called the "City of Lights" as the sun set and the only light source came from the fires that still burned throughout the city. As he looked back and forth confused, he spoke up again.

"You said this was Paris, but I don't see the Eiffel Tower."

Taurus merely swung his arm out wide and pointed to a blank space on the skyline where twisted, broken metal still smoldered low to the ground. Like magic, the younger man's eyes lit up, his vision sharpened and focused like those of a falcon, and he could see clearly and with almost binocular vision the smoldering remains of the Iron Lady. She lay to rest in pieces, her parts being stripped by the dark demonic creatures that now crawled over every rooftop in Paris.

The younger man, Jude, "The Prophet" as Taurus kept referring to him as, a tall man but thin and of meek stature, watched in horror as his eyes, now enhanced by whatever other worldly power wielded by his new teacher, could clearly make out the terrible creatures in the distance. Some were covered in thick fur and walked on all fours, and resembled wolves if not for the very human front facing eyes and near hairless heads. Even with wolves' snouts they still looked like some amalgamation of a man and beast, crudely assembled in the darkest parts of one's nightmares.

Jude watched, unable to speak, as they tore at brick and mortar as though it were nothing. Their claws ripped into steal as easily as they ripped into flesh and they tore both apart to serve some dark and horrendous purpose. Before his eyes, now enhanced, he saw groups digging through the surface as they tried to create a hole in the center of the city.

"Prophet," Taurus bellowed, shocking Jude out of his trance. "We must leave before they reach the city's catacombs."

Jude turned on his heels and followed down the rubble after Taurus.

"Why? What would they want with old dead bones? If they wanted dead bodies there's plenty aroun..." Jude cut himself off as he realized quickly that he was flippantly talking about hundreds of thousands of residents of Paris now dead in the streets.

Taurus either did not pick up on the reference or did not care. Either way, he kept walking, leading Jude out of the city.

"There are more than human remains buried in the catacombs of Paris. He is also buried there."

"Who?" Jude asked while they quickened their pace, as the smoke grew farther and farther into the distance.

"One conquered long ago. One you cannot face, that is not your purpose."

"Speaking of that," Jude tried to talk and keep up with the Zodiac as best he could, "you never mentioned exactly what my purpose is. You just keep going on calling me 'The Prophet' but you haven't really explained what that means."

At this, Taurus stopped and turned so quickly that Jude almost ran into him. He looked down at Jude causing him to crane his neck to look back up at the massive man. It had only been a few days since the Zodiac appeared, seemingly out of thin air, and announced that Jude was The Prophet. Excited to leave a somewhat dull life Jude jumped at the chance for adventure, even if he thought himself half mad to believe a two and a half meter tall supernatural being was towering over him in his bedroom.

But in the course of a few days, the entire civilized world exploded into war. While many news outlets were screaming about World War III, the video and images being captured depicted a non-human threat.

"I did warn you that many major civilizations before you have been cleared from the Earth, did I not?" Taurus now seemed even more intimidating than before.

"Well yea, but…"

"You see the very destruction before your eyes, yes?"

"See, yes. Believe, not so sure…"

"Then why waste precious minutes seeking answers to questions when the world burns?" Taurus' eyes now burnt into Jude's mind and soul. It was as though he didn't want a verbal answer to the question at all, but would rather search the thoughts of his pupil and find the answers himself.

Jude stared back, desperate to hear the Zodiac tell him what this mysterious destiny was all about. But instead the eternal being stared right back for long moments that went on forever while, like Taurus said, the world burned. Jude's eyes began to water as he realized he could not blink, he could not even look away. His gaze was caught by the Zodiac, and it would not be given back until Taurus was satisfied.

But it wasn't only his sight that was deadlocked, his breath wasn't coming at all either. As if his lungs had forgotten how to work or just decided to give up. Jude began to panic for a moment, neither able to look away nor draw breath. He wondered if his heart would give out too, or that perhaps none of this was real and he would wake up in his small bed in his small apartment, face down on his pillow. At least that would explain the lack of breathing.

From his peripheral vision he noticed the scene around them changing. Although his sight was still locked on Taurus' enchanting eyes, he could make out the sky changing colors from dark and grey to lighter, even with a spot of white clouds here and there. Then Jude was almost certain he saw a seagull fly past Taurus behind his head.

Then, suddenly, his breath returned. Jude gasped and panted for air, fell to his knees and clutched his hands over his sore eyes.

"What did you do to me?!" he demanded.

"Do? Nothing. We merely traveled. It can be…a jarring experience for humans." Taurus said, as he turned his attention towards the ocean.

Jude squinted through his watering eyes and found they were now on a beach, the sound of waves filled his ears and gone were the smells of burnt bread and smoke. Still squinting, he managed to get to his feet and turned in a full circle to look at his new surroundings. He stumbled up next to Taurus, who was staring out at the water.

"Where are we?" Jude asked.

"You know it as Greece. I have much history here. This is a good place to start."

"Start what?"

"You are The Prophet. You must learn from the past, and take heed of the future. You cannot understand where this world is going, unless you see where it's been. Are you ready to begin, Prophet?"

Jude shook his head and ran a hand through his hair.

"Yea, I guess. Can you just do me one favor though? Call me Jude."

"No," Taurus said firmly.

"Yeah. Thought I'd at least ask."

The night shift was always Samantha's favorite. Something about working in the day when everyone was up and about didn't suit her as well. It's not that she didn't like people, she loved people. She never would have gotten into this line of work had she not had an affinity for helping others. But there was something more peaceful about the night shift that made her excited about work. As a paramedic, that was an invaluable trait to have.

Tonight of course was a different matter all together. Word had spread of some kind of terrorist attack in Paris. Social media was abuzz with pictures and images of the city burning and bodies piled in the streets. Some said it was a nuclear blast, some said it was a suicide bomber, and still others said an alien invasion. But no one in the States seemed to know for sure what was happening, or if they did they weren't saying.

Then came the panic. She and her partner had responded to three calls already of attempted suicide where the victim thought for sure the world was about to end. Luckily, the attempts on all counts were flimsy and failed, but Samantha worried that the panic might escalate to rioting as the night went on.

"You've been unusually quiet," her partner Josh said, as she stared out the passenger window of the ambulance.

"Hmmm? Oh, just thinking about, stuff and things I guess." Samantha replied.

"Care to share with your partner?" Josh prodded. Samantha shrugged.

"All this Paris stuff. Have you been keeping up on it at all?"

"Nah, not really. France was never really my thing. The ex-wife and I honeymooned in Hong Kong. That was an experience. Not the most romantic of places but the food was really something else."

Samantha turned away from the window to give her partner a disapproving look.

"What?" Josh asked, feeling the stare of judgement.

"You know Paris is under attack, right?"

"Oh, yeah that. Yeah that's horrible." Samantha continued to glare at him as he tried to change the subject, however before either of them could say another word the radio came to life.

"All units we have a possible MI at 55th and Ray Street. Patient is a sixty-two year old Hispanic male. Code Three."

Samantha quickly grabbed the radio and barked into it while Josh flipped on the lights and sirens and made a hard right turn.

"Dispatch, Unit zero-three-zero responding. We've got this one, over." Samantha said, pointing out the front windshield and gave Josh directions. "Take a left at March Street, it runs right into 55th."

"You know this neighborhood well?" Josh asked, expertly weaving through traffic.

"I grew up downtown. We used to play on the basketball courts on 49th."

"Basketball? I thought you'd be more of a tennis gal."

Samantha chuckled, punched Josh in the arm, and finally smiled. "Tennis? Yeah right. No way you're ever going to catch me in one of those stupid uniforms."

Josh snickered back as he made a hard left turn, Samantha smiling as the ambulance whirled around a street corner. The smile faded quickly, though, as Samantha suddenly saw a woman only a few meters away standing in the middle of the road. She looked out of place in her Victorian attire, complete with golden armor adorning her outfit.

"Watch out!" Samantha yelled, as she braced her arms on the dashboard of the vehicle. Without slowing down at all, Josh seemingly ran over the woman in the road, though she neither moved nor did the ambulance hit her. Samantha frantically looked over the hood of the car to see no signs of an impact.

"Whoa, are you ok?" asked Josh as he maneuvered the ambulance down the next street. "You kind of scared me back there. What was that about?"

"You didn't see that woman in the road?!"

"Noooo, and neither did you. There's wasn't anybody there Samantha, just calm down, take a deep breath. We're almost there. Tell me about the ghost lady after we save this next guy, ok?"

She couldn't answer, so Samantha just nodded in agreement instead.

"Geez, you really do need a day off don't you?" Samantha, now fully awake and alert, nodded her head as the ambulance pulled to a stop.

By the time they got out, the large Hispanic man had a small crowd around him and had been laid on his back.

"Stand aside! Move aside please!" Samantha announced loudly as she and Josh pushed their way to the center of the small crowd. "What happened? Did anyone see?"

"I just found him there groaning," said a skinny man, no older than twenty-five, in baggy pants and a ball cap. "I came out of the club and here he was. I think he was in there for a while too."

Samantha quickly looked up to see the neon lights of a strip club. The "club" the skinny man was talking about. She tried not to show her disapproval, now wasn't the time. Though she thought, perhaps, a man with a heart condition shouldn't be having too much excitement.

The pair began working on the man immediately like clockwork and with very little conversation between the two. This wasn't their first heart attack patient and they knew time was most certainly a factor.

As Samantha worked she noticed everything began to slow down a bit, as if time was, for once at least, working on their side. Her eyes darted quickly between the man and her kit, her hands moved without being told where to go and what to do. For an instant, just one instant, she could almost feel the man being healed. She looked down and caught his gaze, a stunned, scared look gripped her. Samantha's hands moved in slow motion, compressing his chest. She felt a warm glow begin to swell in her elbows and radiate down to her wrists, then her hands.

And then he was gone.

The body was loaded into a coroner's van just as Josh finished putting his signature on the paperwork. Samantha sat on the back end of the ambulance, rubbing her own shoulders as though trying to rub away sore memories.

"You ok?" Josh asked.

"Yeah, I'm ok. I really thought we had this one. Like, for a moment there I could almost…I don't know."

"Almost what?" Josh prodded.

"Almost felt him coming out of it. Ya know? And then bam! He's dead."

"That's how it happens", Josh said as he looked down at his watch. "Fifteen minutes and shift is up. Why don't we call it a day? You can come over to my place, we can grab a drink…"

Samantha gave a weak laugh.

"Yeah right. Last time we went over to your place for a drink after work you didn't make it to the fridge."

"Well, we can do that too," he smiled.

"Not tonight. I've got...I don't know, something else on my mind. Not tonight."

"So speaking of something else, what was with that ghost lady you saw on the way here?"

Samantha stood from the ambulance and shook her head, then rested her forehead in her palm as she paced a little.

"I have no idea. I could have sworn I saw a woman standing in the middle of road. And, and the weirdest thing, she wasn't wearing normal clothes."

Josh raised an eyebrow and moved closer. "Not normal clothes? Like what then? Was she dressed like a clown or something?"

"No, but like, almost like renaissance faire garb. Red and gold and I think she was wearing armor..." Josh nodded, unbelievingly.

"Yeah you're right, you don't need a drink. You need sleep. I'll drive, let's get back to the hospital."

With that, the two closed up the ambulance doors and drove off into the night.

In the shadows, watching closely, stood a tall figure dressed in intricately designed Victorian clothing, arms and legs adorned with golden armor. She watched carefully as the ambulance disappeared from sight. Then, as though she was never there, she vanished.

Chapter 2

Samantha's apartment was small and old, but even with the lack of natural light, and not much of a view to speak of, it had a boutique type of charm that hit her the moment she first saw it. And here, four years later, she still enjoyed coming home to her quaint little castle in the city. She was greeted by her black cat, Buddy, who had just gotten up himself at hearing her come through the door and was ready to be fed.

"Hey you," she said in a higher pitched voice than what she'd address a person in. "How was your day? Ok, ok, I'll go first. So…" she began listing out the events of her work day while she opened a can of food for the cat. Buddy delightfully purred his acceptance while he ate and listened to Samantha divulge the details of her day.

Being a paramedic meant that she had to work odd hours which left very little time for socializing. When the rest of the world was awake, she was asleep. That also left little time for grocery shopping, going to the bank, or performing any tasks that a nine-to-five type of job would have allowed. But she made due, and enjoyed it just the same.

"And then," she continued with Buddy, "we turned down one street and I'm not kidding there was this woman in weird clothes standing right in the road! But we drove right into her and, poof, nothing. It's like she was a ghost."

"I'm not a ghost," said the tall woman in the strange clothes, who now stood in Samantha's living room directly behind her. Samantha jumped, screamed, and scared Buddy who ran off into the bedroom. She tripped over her small coffee table and tumbled to the floor.

"Holy crap! Holy crap who are you?! How did you get in here!?" She demanded, while looking for something with which to defend herself.

"I'm not a ghost," the woman repeated. "Please be calm, allow me to explain." Immediately Samantha was calm, she breathed normally and though on high alert, she was able to stand to her feet and stay still.

"I am Aries, the Ram, The Zodiac, a Timeless one. And you, Samantha Riley, are The Healer." Aries announced.

"Oh. Okay. Sure." Samantha said and she slowly sat down on her couch, stunned. "So I haven't been getting enough sleep lately, already addressed that. Lack of sleep, mixed with improper diet, perfect cocktail for hallucinations."

"You are not hallucinating, Samantha."

"Of course I'm not. I'm talking to a…" Samantha looked Aries up and down, taking note of her usual height, "I'm talking to a six and half, maybe seven foot warrior looking chick in my living room who appeared out of nowhere. But no, I'm not hallucinating."

Aries took a step forward, causing Samantha to back into her couch and crane her neck to look at the tall woman.

"You have a special purpose, Samantha. Unfortunately, there isn't much time for me to explain everything, so this will have to suffice." Aries gently reached out a hand, covered in a gold gauntlet with fine designs etched into it and inlaid with rubies of various sizes.

She gently laid her massive palm on Samantha's head, and in an instant her eyes were filled with stars. A tear rolled down Samantha's cheek as her mouth lay agape. Aries took a deep breath and closed her own eyes before removing her hand from Samantha's head, causing her to gasp for air as her body tried to catch up with the thoughts racing in her mind.

"What...did you...just do to...me?" Samantha gasped.

"I showed you what you need to know. A piece of it, for now. Your mind cannot accept the full truth of things all at once." Aries backed away a few steps, giving Samantha room to breathe.

"What...are you? That thing...I just saw...like a memory of...of something. I've never been there before."

"But you have," Aries said calmly, soothingly. "it only looks very different today. I showed you what it was. And what it must be again."

Samantha buried her face in her hands, her mind still reeling from the sudden surprise, and information being downloaded into her brain by a woman claiming to be a supernatural entity. It was almost too much.

"What do you want from me?" She managed to choke out.

"The end of an age is coming. Civilization must make a choice. Continue on, and prosper. Or die, and be reborn."

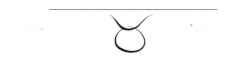

"You realize that's incredibly morbid, right?" Jude asked as he walked along with Taurus. They had been walking for hours by now, and although hunger had set in a while ago, Jude was perfectly fine continuing on, so long as the answers kept coming from the Zodiac.

"To you," Taurus answered without looking at the little human. "Your perspective is framed by your experiences. I must reframe it, so you may see the entire picture, or most of it, better."

"Right, but to say the world is going to end and millions will die and it's all on my shoulders, that just sounds morbid."

"I did not say it's all on your shoulders."

"You did. You literally said," Jude puffed out his chest and deepened his voice, in attempt to mimic Taurus. "What happens next is laid upon your shoulders."

"Yes. Your shoulders, not your shoulders."

"That doesn't make any sense."

Taurus, for the first time in hours, stopped walking and turned to face Jude.

"Prophet," he began.

"Jude," Jude retorted.

"Prophet. Your duty is an imperative one. But the fate of all things does not rest upon your shoulders alone. It rests upon your shoulders, as in humanity's shoulders. We are well aware no one man can save a civilization." At this, Taurus gave the slightest smirk before he turned and kept walking.

"Oh. Well, you could have just said that."

There was silence after that for nearly an hour, with the only sounds being that of the sea and the two very different footstep patterns. Jude was not really accustom to walking this much, and definitely not in his sandals, but those were the only shoes he had with him when Taurus had appeared and whisked him away. They had walked from somewhere on the northern side of the southern peninsula of Greece, over dirt roads and eventually trails through a canyon and now again along the cliffs overlooking the sea. But for the life of him Jude had no idea where they actually were, and his mobile phone had long since died.

The view, however, was spectacular. And the conversation had greatly improved with his tour guide, even if the subject was of the death and destruction of the entire modern world. Jude hadn't really accepted this, save for the sights of Paris burning before his eyes, and the unexplained phenomenon of the creatures tearing the Eiffel Tower to pieces. Somewhere in his head, though, he believed he would wake up from this very vivid dream and swear off whatever food he had eaten before going to bed.

"We're almost there," said Taurus, breaking the silence.

"Oh good, I was wondering when we were finally going to get there," Jude responded in jest.

"Next I must show you a piece of ancient past. It will be hard for you to fathom, but you must see it anyhow."

"Wait, are we talking like the thing you did to me in Paris? Where I saw all those monsters?"

"No."

"Oh good," Jude breathed a sigh of relief. "'Cause I didn't appreciate that one bit."

Page 18

"What you saw in Paris was the present. I must show you the past."

"But the same head trip you pulled?"

"No."

"Oh good."

"Before, I adjusted your eyes. This time, I will adjust your mind."

Jude breathed a heavy sigh. He wasn't so sure he should even continue asking questions at all, given the answers that were coming his way.

"So, what exactly are you going to show me? The history of Greece?" He prodded.

"No," Taurus answered coldly. "The history of a civilization that failed, where you must try and succeed."

"And which civilization is that?"

"Atlantis." Taurus said as he stepped up onto a small pony wall at the edge of the dirt road. He looked over the waters toward the islands off the coast.

"Wait, did you say Atlantis?" Jude followed him onto the wall, looking out over the sea as though he might spot evidence of the mythical city in the blue waters.

"I did." Taurus said, his eyes looking down at Jude and making note of the sudden enthusiasm.

"But Atlantis was just a myth. It wasn't an actual, real place." Jude said, with a glimmer of hope behind the statement that he may be wrong.

"Hours ago you did not believe in the demonic creatures that tore Paris to pieces. An hour from now, you will be the only living person in an age to have real knowledge of the lost city."

Jude began to get excited, even a little hopeful that perhaps this wasn't a strange taco-induced dream after all.

"But I thought Atlantis was, you know, in the Atlantic Ocean? Aren't we still in Greece?"

"We are. But it was not. Not permanently, anyhow."

The pair stopped at the southern most tip of the Greek peninsula. Jude looked out over the waters, in the distance were the Greek Isles, he could barely see over the blue waters.

"It's beautiful," he said, gazing up at Taurus for a response.

"Then let us hope it stays this way," Taurus said. "What must come next will seem very odd to you. Do not fear, your feet will never leave this stone. Only your mind will drift into the past."

"Well let's drift away then. I can't wait to…"

But he was cut off as Taurus placed a palm on the back of Jude's head. Out of the clear blue sky, and not far off in the distance, came a boulder the size of a house, crashing into the ocean. The initial splash shot up several meters into the air and the resulting wave rushed the cliffs where they both stood.

Jude ducked at first and jumped back as the wave came closer but didn't climb high enough to reach them on the pony wall.

"What was that?!" he exclaimed.

Moments later, more rock fragments, smaller than the first but easily the size of cars each, tumbled from the sky and splashed into the water. Jude focused for a minute on the first big chunk and could make out just before it sunk completely, what looked like a white tower on the rock. He turned his eyes up and his jaw down as he noticed where the rocks were all coming from.

Emerged from the wispy clouds was a massive island that flew over their heads and headed due East. Behind it was a trail of dark black smoke that came from somewhere on top of the island. Jude could make out sections of the bottom that appeared to glow an eerie teal color. Though the island was flying, it was also, most definitely, coming apart along the way.

"That...that can't be possible." Jude stammered.

"But it was," Taurus sighed, "and it was magnificent," he added. "Here I show you the fall. Let me take you back just before."

Suddenly Jude's feet left the ground, or so it seemed, and he was lifted high into the air, into and even above the clouds, and suddenly, on solid ground again. He nearly fell over but caught himself by grabbing Taurus' clothing. The Zodiac did not approve, but said nothing. Once he had steadied himself, Jude looked around and found his surroundings completely changed.

They were standing on a terrace high above a fantastic, Roman styled city. From where they stood, he couldn't really tell that they were not on solid ground, at least not on the Earth.

"Atlantis, a city of marvels," Taurus began. "None like it before, and none since. Plato wrote about it as an island joining North America and Africa. He was only half right, however. Atlantis was a city of trade, and it ferried goods from continent to continent. It often made port in Africa, North America, and part of modern Europe."

"This is unbelievable," Jude gawked as he approached the edge of the terrace and looked down. Beneath them were stacked piles an piles of perfectly chiseled stone.

"Those stones, they're huge. I've seen them before."

"You've seen some similar. Atlantis provided the Pharaohs of Egypt with hewn stone for their pyramids."

"Oh come on! Seriously? Everyone knows the pyramids were built by aliens," Jude teased, watching Taurus out of the corner of his eye.

"They were not, in fact. But we Zodiac are sometimes mistaken as such." Taurus pointed out over the terrace at another large man in elegant robes similar to those of everyone else, walking with a middle-aged man in common attire.

"Look there," Taurus pointed, "you'll see one of my companions. Aquarius, the Cup Bearer, walking with his steward."

Aquarius walked and spoke with the middle-aged man then paused and looked up toward the terrace. He smiled and gave a gentle nod to Taurus, who replied with an outstretched arm. Aquarius continued walking and speaking while Jude turned to Taurus.

"You said you were just showing me the past, how can he see you?"

"We Timeless are outside of time. You see a moment that has long since been, but I come and go throughout time freely. This moment we now stand in contains the moments before the sundering of Atlantis."

"If you were here, and Aquarius was here, why couldn't you stop it?"

"It was not for us to stop."

"Why not? I can hardly believe this was real, a real floating island?! And you didn't stop it from being destroyed?" Jude turned away from the terrace and now faced Taurus full on.

"Our charge is not to protect civilization from the coming storm. We are only here to observe and to train those who might protect it from the enemy that wishes to tear it apart."

Jude breathed an exasperated sigh and rested his arms on the stone railing.

"Tell me about this place."

"Atlantis. A city of marvels, none like it before..."

"Yes I got that part. What else? Why was it so marvelous? How in the hell did they make an island fly?"

"I cannot divulge the details of their technology. Nor would you understand it. Neither could they understand the mobile phone in your pocket, nor the computer at your desk. They have no reference to comprehend the internet. Nor do you have reference to understand what they called the Lantern Stones they have smelted together that help propel the city upward."

"The what? Go back what was that last part?" Jude pulled out his phone to take notes, only to realize it was still dead.

"This civilization thrived, and advanced well beyond what was thought possible in this age. Yet all they had achieved was no more than tying a shoelace together compared to what they were about to discover. But, it was not to be."

A loud explosion rocked the courtyard below and shook the terrace on which Taurus and Jude stood. They both looked over the edge to see the chaos below, and Jude bobbed his head to try to see through the black smoke curling upwards towards them.

"It is he." Taurus said coldly.

"The same guy that was in Paris?" Jude asked, eyes wide and trying to get a better look.

"No. Far worse. He has not yet appeared in your time, though he will. He is the Chaotic One. The Destroyer. Apollyon."

Chapter 3

♈

Samantha walked uneasily through the halls of her hospital, in hopes of making it to the locker room, or a bathroom, before she was sick in the hallway. Her encounter with the seven-foot tall woman that called herself Aries along with everything she said to Samantha about the end of the world coming, had her stomach in knots.

She made it to the lockers and sat down on a bench to breathe deeply and get her mind off of things. It was of course perfectly reasonable that she hallucinated the entire event. She was working long night shifts and not sleeping much during the day after all. It certainly wasn't beyond the scope of her imagination.

Why a giant woman in renaissance clothing though? She thought. *And what was with the armor? That wasn't from any movie I saw or book I read lately. Come on Sam, there's a perfectly good explanation for all this.*

"Of course there is," Aries said, suddenly standing next to Samantha in the otherwise empty locker room. Samantha jumped but managed to keep from screaming this time.

"The explanation is I am real, and everything I told you is the truth," Aries smiled down at her.

"Were you…reading my thoughts?" Samantha asked incredulously.

"No. I was listening to them. They're quite loud."

Samantha drug her nails through her hair.

"This isn't happening. You're not real," She repeated over and over.

"Healer, as I told you before, time is short if you're going to get ahead of the Chaos. We need to go." Aries was calm and collected but there was a sense of urgency to her voice as well that Samantha had heard time and time again with patients.

When laying on a sidewalk, or being hoisted onto a gurney, often a patient would speak calmly and cooly to Samantha and her partner Josh. But there was a tone of panic, of worry, of doubt, and always of fear associated with it as well. It took Samantha a few years to be able to discern the difference between true calm, and the facade so many put on when they try to tell themselves everything will be okay, but deep inside they know if they have any chance of survival, the speed and talent of this paramedic will truly be the difference between life and death.

It was this way with Aries now.

She may seem calm, and collected and she spoke earlier of the many ages that have passed before her eyes. But there was a sense of urgency that betrayed the calm in her voice. And it was that, which Samantha now sensed, and that would drive her next choice.

"Ok, let's say just for giggles I believe you. Let's say I'm not sleep deprived and you are some supernatural giant woman that only I can see. Assuming all that's true, what now?"

"Africa," Aries said plainly.

"Africa? You want me to go to Africa?"

"I will take you there, yes."

"Will you at least tell me why?"

"There is a stone deep beneath Lake Victoria, placed there by an emissary from Egypt. The stone itself is priceless, but it is also tainted. Centuries ago, when chaos reigned in the hearts of kings and Pharaohs, a gift was given that was meant to destroy the whole continent of Africa.

"A greedy, arrogant king had his most trusted servants take the stone in the middle of the night, after a celebratory feast when all slept, drunk and full. They traveled across the desert for weeks and then dropped the stone into the bottom of the lake. They would head back to tell only their king of it's location, but the taint was already upon them. In the end, their bones were buried in the sands of the Sahara.

"Meanwhile, Pharaoh was enraged at the betrayal, and waged war against the king. Both their armies suffered immeasurable losses and millions died. Parchments containing the wisdom and knowledge of all Egypt were burned when the halls of the scribes of Pharaoh were sacked. Scholars were blinded and their tongues were cut out, so they could not continue the histories they once protected.

"A great and thriving civilization was torn to pieces, over the greed of a few men, and the demonic taint in that cursed stone."

Samantha stayed silent a moment, captivated by the mere telling of the story. Whether or not any of it was true was irrelevant. The story itself completely grabbed her imagination and wonder about a distant time in a far off land.

"So, you want me to...find this stone?"

"No," Aries said flatly. "The stone has already been discovered. Within days the lake bed will be dredged and the stone brought to the surface. It will be heralded as a wonder, and wealthy men and women and dignitaries from all over the earth will come to marvel at, and touch, the stone. And they will return home carrying the taint with them, and infecting their loved ones, and their servants and employees and families. And the world will rot."

"My god, are you serious? Well I don't want to go near that thing!"

"You are The Healer, Samantha. I will take you to the only item on this planet that can stop the taint. This is your charge. You are one of twelve chosen to fight against the coming Chaos, and the one who would see not only this civilization, but also this world turn to ash."

Samantha slowly stood, still dwarfed by the massive Zodiac, and held out her hand. It was awkward but it seemed like the right thing to do.

"Ok, then. If everything you're telling me is true, I'll believe you. Let's do this."

Aries smiled broadly, placed a ruby encrusted golden gauntlet on Samantha's shoulder, and the next instant the locker room was empty.

"The enemy has many weapons," Taurus raised his voice over the noise of screams, fire and explosions. "He uses greed, pride, lust, which are all very standard, against the hearts of powerful men to create the Chaos."

Taurus stepped over chunks of rubble like they were pebbles, while Jude was having a harder time dodging debris. He attempted to wave away smoke that limited his vision, but the smoke would not obey his hands.

"That's no good, you're not really here. Only a memory."

"But you're here! How is it you can interact with this, but I can't?!" Jude yelled over the noise.

"Because I *am* here." Taurus stooped to gently pick up a man in grey and teal robes, a resident of Atlantis. He carried him through a portcullis and just outside the outer courtyard. They had reached an edge of the floating island, pieces had not yet begun falling off, and the wind almost knocked Jude over as he stepped into the open.

"Where are we?" Jude asked, shielding his face from the brisk wind.

"Still over the Atlantic. There's an army in Northern Africa they'll try to reach. But by the time they get close, the island will have begun to fall apart."

There was a sudden fierce shake. Jude dropped to all fours to steady himself but Taurus didn't budge. When the shaking stopped he stooped again and laid the man onto the grass.

"M-m-mercy. Save us," the man gasped.

"It'll be over soon. Be at peace," Taurus said smoothly, the very words made Jude feel like he could fall asleep where he stood and dream for one thousand years. Then he snapped back to his senses.

"Wait a minute!" He marched over to Taurus who now stood and met him off the grass. "If you can pick that guy up, and he can see you, why can't you help these people?"

"This man is close to death. The veil between this world and another is thin. He will not survive to tell of what he has seen."

"Still! People are dying in there!"

"Those people are dead, Prophet. In this time, your greatest ancestors have not yet been born. There is no helping these people now. But there are billions in your time that will die if the Chaos is not stopped. I show you only the past, but you can take hold of the present."

Jude shook his head and buried his face in his hands.

"What can I possibly do against this?! You saw what they did in Paris. And they didn't even have this...apple... Appl-yon..."

"Apollyon." Taurus corrected.

"Yeah him! So how am I supposed to stop all this?"

"There are others. But they must be brought together."

The island shook again, but this time, some fifty meters away, a piece of rock on the edge, no bigger than a city bus, cracked and fell away from the main island.

"Ah, it's begun. We should go."

"Wait...you showed me that other guy. What was his name, Aquarius! He's here in this time walking with someone from this time. Can't they stop all this?"

Taurus frowned and shook his head.

"This would be Aquarius' great failure. After this he vanished into the depths of the galaxy for some time, and would not show his face again for several ages. And he has not carried out his charge since the fall of Atlantis."

They walked to the edge of the island, wispy clouds in the air, nothing but the distant sea below. Taurus snapped his fingers and the ground beneath them broke from the island. Gravity took hold of the island first, and Jude felt his stomach rise up in his throat as his body caught on.

They fell.

Clouds passed, and wind rushed by over the expanse of the ocean, while pieces of Atlantis broke, falling beneath them as they fell. Jude squinted his eyes as the wind made it hard for him to keep them open, and suddenly he was sprayed in the face with salty, ocean water.

There they stood atop the sea wall at the southern most tip of Greece. As Taurus had promised, Jude's feet never left the ground where he stood. That didn't keep him from thrashing about, though, as he expected to be in the Atlantic Ocean by now.

Nearby, some small children laughed and pointed, having watched a high wave crash into the cliff and having seen Jude's reaction to getting a face full of ocean spray. Taurus laughed as well, though only Jude saw or heard him. He stood up and looked around frantically, and after a moment having realized where and when he was, collapsed onto the wall.

"Not funny," he muttered.

"We are not without a sense of humor. And that was humorous!" Taurus bellowed.

"You did that on purpose." Jude pouted.

After much more laughter from the Zodiac, he joined Jude sitting on the sea wall.

"As I was saying," he began, "Aquarius was deeply damaged by the destruction of Atlantis. There are some among us that harbor anger towards him for not discharging his duty. But we hold no ill will towards him."

"So what, was he in charge of that...timeline's prophet?" Jude asked, tying to make sense of things.

"No, he was tasked with preparing The Warrior. Each age we are given a task, a man or woman to find who will serve a great purpose in the protection of their civilization."

"So if he hasn't been doing his job, does that mean no Warrior?"

"One of us has taken the slack each age. There must be twelve."

"Right, twelve Zodiac, twelve of us special people then, huh? What about Gemini? Are there two of them?"

"The Twins take on only one steward." Taurus seemed a little miffed at this, enough so for Jude to notice.

"Slackers huh? I got ya."

They both sat in silence again for a few minutes, listening to and watching the waves pound against the cliffs. Behind them children played and overhead gulls complained. In this moment it would have been hard to believe Paris was burning.

"So will I meet the other eleven then?" Jude asked, still looking out at the sea.

"That is your destiny." Jude turned sharp and gave Taurus his full attention.

"What? Am I their leader or something?"

"Hardly. You see what has been, and what is, and what will come. You guide, but you do not lead. You instruct, but you do not command. In this puzzle there are many pieces, and none less important than the other."

"Hmmmmm," Jude rubbed his face and nodded in thought. "But I bring them all together?"

"Yes."

"Awesome. So who is our warrior then?"

Riku Yatsukura considered himself a warrior. Even his name spelled in kanji was written as "spring tiger", which caused his grandparents to nickname him "little tiger". At age six, his grandfather began teaching him Kendo in their family dojo just outside Kyoto, Japan.

His grandfather was a loving old man that cared deeply for his family. He had seen the horrors of war during World War II and though he rarely spoke of it to Riku, he insisted on teaching his grandson to be strong and to practice the ways of the sword.

As a young boy Riku dreamed of one day going to war and slicing through his enemy with his grandfather's katana. But when his grandfather died his own father donated the sword to a Museum for Japanese History.

"That sword is only a reminder of a darker time," his father would say to him.

Still it didn't dissuade Riku from his practice and study. After high school he moved to Tokyo for college and got a job cleaning a local Kendo dojo. It was much more modern than the one he was accustom to back home, but at least he was able to practice without the judging eye of his father.

After practicing he would change clothes and mop the floor, put away the floor mats, arrange the shinai and make sure the dojo was ready for the next class. His payment was received in free training time and free classes at the dojo. An arrangement greatly accepted by the owner and sensei of the dojo when Riku had made the proposal to him.

His duties done for the day, Riku grabbed his bag and headed for the door, when he heard footsteps. No, not footsteps; horse steps. Very clearly coming from outside the building, Riku swore he heard horse hooves clomping steadily in his direction. Louder and louder they grew and loser and closer they came. Then, they stopped.

Riku put his ear to the door and listened carefully for any sounds or indication that he wasn't simply hearing things. But then the noise began again and only got louder until he was certain if he opened the door there would in fact be a horse, and hopefully a rider, standing on the other side.

Cautiously he pulled the door back enough to allow him to peek out. No horse, no rider, just the usual Tokyo street traffic and a few cars here and there. Curious he closed the door again and paused a moment, and listened for more hoof sounds.

But none came.

Riku shrugged and went to leave when, very clearly, he heard a horse whinny directly behind him. He spun, shocked to see a massive black steed towering over him and in the saddle what appeared to be a giant in full samurai armor staring down at him. The horse pawed at the floor with both hooves but didn't seem to scratch or mark the wooden floor.

Riku shrieked and bolted from the door around to the far end of the dojo, bracing himself against the wall. The giant samurai slowly dismounted the horse, which remained perfectly still afterwards, and faced Riku. Attached to the side of the saddle was a long, red yumi, a Japanese long bow that ran almost the full length of the horse itself.

The samurai squared off against Riku and straightened himself, then bowed before the tiny human.

Riku, both shocked and somewhat excited, bowed as well, keeping his eyes on the giant. Then the samurai reached for his side and slowly drew a long, dark brown bokken.

Riku's jaw dropped.

"This can't be real," he said.

The samurai swiftly raised the wooden sword and brought it down against Riku's deltoid with a snap. Not quite hard enough to cause damage, but hard enough to jolt Riku out of his stupor.

"Ow!" he hollered. "You're...you're real!?" Riku stammered, backing against the wall and knocking over several weapons. He hastily grabbed the first thing he could, a bamboo shinai, and faced his giant opponent.

"Look I don't know what you are, or why you're here..."

He didn't get to finish his sentence before the samurai struck again. This time Riku deflected the blow, but just barley, and the force of the impact nearly knocked him his off his feet.

"Hey! Whoa! Say something!" He yelled at the giant.

Behind the samurai's face mask his eyes burned with fire. He raised the bokken again to strike, but this time was met with a now furious Riku. With a shout he began striking the samurai over and over, albeit doing little damage, with the bamboo sword. The samurai smiled behind the mask and began his own volley of attacks, each met with the bamboo sword in Riku's hands.

The two engaged blow after blow whilst moving around all over the newly washed wooden floor, as the large black steed stood off to the side watching and occasionally throwing it's head about in approval.

Finally Riku landed a near contact hit against the side of the samurai's face, Riku having to stretch his arms to the limit just to reach. The samurai froze, then backed up and stood straight. Riku followed suit.

The samurai sheathed his bokken, the sword then vanished all together, and he bowed again. Riku cautiously bowed back. The samurai slowly reached up and removed the helmet and mask revealing short black hair and the stone colored face of a man. His eyes still burned with fire, flames occasionally flickered beyond where the eyelids should be and looked as though it might burn his eyebrows, but did not.

"Riku Yatsukura," he began in a voice that resounded like one hundred waterfalls, "I am Sagittarius, the Archer, the Timeless Zodiac. I have come to find you, to test you, and to train you to fulfill your destiny as The Warrior."

Riku stood motionless a moment, the shinai fell from his hand to the floor as he stared up at Sagittarius. His gaped mouth slowly curled upward into the most ridiculous smile any young man has ever given.

"Yes!" he cried out with excitement.

Chapter 4

Night had fallen on the City of Lights in more ways than one. Any remaining living inhabitants of Paris had either run or been evacuated, which left the only presence remaining that of the Dark Ones. The foul smelling, wolf-like creatures with the heads and eyes of men and the snouts of canines. They worked in packs like wolves, tearing apart the remains of of the Eiffel Tower, stacking the corpses of the fallen denizens of Paris, and digging up the streets towards their underground goal.

After hours of flinging dirt into the air a pack of a dozen or so broke through the underground cavern ceiling and collapsed into the a dark tunnel. They recovered quickly and peered around, the darkness was no inhibitor to their sight. There, human skulls lined the walls of the famous catacombs of Paris. The creatures grinned and howled their delight at having reached their goal.

Now was the next and meticulous task of finding the pieces of their dismembered master, the once feared creature known as The Wicked Man. Throughout the ages, there had been tales of monsters, dragons, the dead come to life, and so on. Most had attributed these to myth, stories that bore no real weight in the realm of reality.

But these were more than mere stories and myths. They were warnings from the ancient and forgotten cultures and peoples that lived through the Chaos, and sought to pass down information for future generations. How unfortunate that those future generations would never heed the advice of their elders. And in failing to do so they themselves fell victim to the Chaos. Age after age, civilization after civilization would fall, and men and women would die for lack of understanding.

They were not without victories, though, those ancestors of old. And one such victory was the destruction of The Wicked Man at the hands of the Chosen. Twelve men and women gathered by the Timeless from across the globe fought against the evil he spread and his army of Dark Ones. In what is now Paris, France, they struck him down and tore his body apart to prevent his return.

Though they eventually lost the war and their age came to and end, they stuck the Chaos a mighty blow by defeating one of the enemy's greatest generals. Centuries later, ancient cemeteries and burial grounds would be exhumed, and the bodies therein moved to the catacombs. The bones of The Wicked Man were dug up with the bodies of others and implanted throughout the underground tunnels and caverns beneath the city.

And now his army returned, to reassemble their warrior general and begin the onslaught anew.

"But I don't understand," Riku complained. "If the battle is in France, why are you sending me to America?" Sagittarius rode along side his tiny steward, mounted atop his great black steed. He had procured a horse for Riku to ride as well from a dude ranch in Saitama.

"The weapon you need is found there, Warrior." The Zodiac answered.

"All I need is good katana and I'm ready to fight! I've been training my whole life for this!"

"A good katana will turn to dust, and a great katana will shatter. You need a sword that has met the enemy before."

"I have never seen a katana turn to dust!" Riku argued.

"You have never seen the claws of a Dark One shred iron like paper."

Riku admitted defeat.

He was beside himself with excitement over his new found title and purpose. He wanted more than anything to hit the battlefield and vanquish the enemy for the honor of his family name. He was ready to fight in a great war, just the his grandfather had. But Sagittarius kept talking to him about training and purpose and someone else he had to work with.

"So what kind of sword do I need to find in America?"

"It belonged to a Viking."

"A Viking sword!? No way a Viking sword is better than a katana!"

"This is no ordinary sword. It once belonged to the greatest warrior of all, the mighty Achilles."

Riku stopped his horse at this.

"Achilles? Like in the Greek myth?"

"The very same," Sagittarius said, more with a sense of pride.

"But he wasn't real."

"He was very real. He was a magnificent student, a mighty warrior. He was a fearsome man with no equal."

"A student? You trained Achilles?"

Page 41

"I did."

"Wait a second, aren't you supposed to be a centaur? A man-horse or something?" Sagittarius grunted at this question.

"Stories evolve. Legends become twisted into myth. But in battle, I fight and ride as though my horse and I are one."

This explanation was more than satisfactory for Riku, it was the truth of the ages finding it's way into his brain. It just made sense. If the Zodiac are real, and their myths are exaggerated stories of the past, then why couldn't other things be true as well.

"How did a Viking get the sword of Achilles?"

"I took him to it, and he lost it in America. Two centuries before Leif Erikson set foot on the North American continent, a clan of Scandinavians set out East across Russia. They traveled seven thousand kilometers before crossing the Bering Strait over the frozen sea.

"Eventually they settled in what the Americans call 'Wyoming'. That is where we are headed."

Riku nodded, drinking in the elaborate tales his mentor told him.

"But the sea isn't frozen anymore. How are we getting there on horseback?"

Sagittarius smiled broadly. He had kept his helmet and mask off as they rode and spoke, and now his smile almost disturbed Riku. He pulled the longbow from his saddle and drew back the bowstring.

"Hold on," he said. An arrow materialized on the bow as he aimed, then he loosed the arrow out towards the horizon. Riku watched the arrow quickly sail out of eyeshot, but suddenly his eyes seemed to catch up to the arrow as it flew.

Riku felt as though his head was being stretched from his neck, and though his legs still sat on the saddle, he thought they might tear from the rest of his body. His eyes were glued on the tail end of the arrow as it soared over land, and then sea as well! He could feel the wind rushing past his ears, could barely make out the sound of his horse whinnying it's displeasure at whatever was happening.

His cheeks flapped in the wind as land approached and soon the ocean was far behind them. The arrow kept flying and began to lose altitude as a large lake came into view. Riku could hear himself screaming as he came to rest, horse and all, on the East end of Yellowstone Lake. The arrow arrived just before him, and was swiftly caught by Sagittarius, who then replaced his bow on his saddle and looked at Riku with a smile.

"Welcome to Wyoming."

Jude stood in line at the Corner Market in the small town of Hulett, Wyoming. He tried to avoid eye contact with anyone else, after he had forgotten that no one else could see the three-meter tall Zodiac that walked with him. So when he spoke out loud to Taurus, he garnered some unusual looks from the locals. They had stopped there, just northeast of Devils Tower, to get a messenger bag, some pens and notebooks. Taurus had offered to collect the items himself stealthily, but

Jude insisted on paying for them. End of the world be damned, he would at least do this the right way.

He stepped up to the clerk, a young girl appearing to be in her twenties. He smiled and placed everything on the counter for her to scan.

"Gettin' ready for college?" the girl asked.

Jude turned a few shades of red and awkwardly rubbed the back of his neck.

"No, uh, I'm just…looking to do some writing."

"Oh you're a writer? What kinda stuff do you write?" she prodded.

"I'm working on a, uh, memoir, I guess you'd call it." He smiled but again tried not to make eye contact with her.

"That's excitin'! You must have a lot to write about bein' so young and all. You in the military or somethin'?"

"No, nothing like that. More history related," he choked out.

"Well, I can't wait to read it," she took his credit card and looked down at the name. "Jude…that's a pretty name. Maybe one day I can say I met the famous writer right here in Hulett."

She bagged his things and pulled a receipt, quickly scrawling something on it and handing it to him.

"Here y'are. You saved three ninety five. Have a nice day, Jude." She winked at him and smiled as he took the bag and the receipt and headed for the door. One more glance to see her helping the next customer caused him to smack his face against the glass of the front door. The girl smiled and waved as he hurried out.

Jude marched across the parking lot towards the road, yanking the messenger bag out and shoving the notebooks and pens inside, completely flustered.

Page 44

"I wouldn't call Jude a 'pretty name'," Taurus commented.

"Shut up," he muttered as they crossed the road.

"You should not be concerned with her…"

"Don't, don't you even begin to tell me she's going to burn, or this land will suffer, or any apocalyptic stuff."

"As you say," Taurus shrugged.

They headed down the road a ways before Jude spoke up again.

"But, she'll be all right won't she?"

"The Dark Ones have no vested interest in Wyoming. Not anymore."

"Anymore?"

"Where we are headed, you must see what has been once more. There is history here."

"Another Chaos, or whatever you call it?"

"Yes."

"What could have possibly happened here? I don't remember reading anything about lost civilizations in Wyoming."

"The history was lost by all except the prophets before you. I do not expect you would have heard their stories as they were passed down orally."

"That makes sense. So where are we headed then?"

Taurus pointed as they rounded the curve of the highway at a strange rock formation that jutted out on the horizon. Nothing in the vicinity even resembled the strange looking protrusion.

"There," he said, "Devils Tower."

"Wait, I know about that place. I remember we learned about in grade school. The Native Americans had a story about sisters that got trapped up there or something."

"Yes."

"And they call it 'Bear Lodge'. Not Devils Tower."

"Most of them, yes. The Kiowa call it 'Tree Rock' and they are more accurate than they know."

"But it's not a tree. It's a volcano. It's rock, right?"

"Now. It was a tree."

Jude stopped walking and stared into the distance at the huge rock formation.

"It something wrong?" Taurus asked.

"No, not really. I'm just waiting for you to do your mind tripping thing. Where I stand here and you take me to the past and I wake up just in time to almost get hit by a car, or have a bird poop on my head. Because that's where this is headed, right?"

Taurus didn't answer, but smiled instead.

Jude watched as the road beneath his feet melted away into dirt and grass. He turned his eyes upward as the stone tower began to change color from a harsh grey into a deep brown. Pockets of lush green began to appear on the sides here and there, and soon the tower itself burst towards the sky.

It grew and grew right before Jude's wide eyes, and suddenly exploded outward with gigantic branches that quickly filled with green leaves. A huge canopy dwarfed the tall trees below it.

"Whoa...now that...is impressive." Jude stood in awe as time worked backwards and the once stone monument became a massive tree.

"Shall we get a closer look?" Taurus asked. He snapped his fingers and the two now stood half a kilometer away on a gentle slope that lead up to the base.

What moments ago was roughly two hundred and sixty meters from base to plateau top, was now easily three times that height in the trunk alone. The canopy extended the height another sixty meters vertically, and the diameter doubled the three hundred meter base.

Even at their distance, Jude had to crane his neck a bit to get the full view of the great tree.

"There was a civilization here?" he asked in awe.

"Is it so hard to believe?" Taurus answered.

"After what you showed me before, not really. So who are they? Ancient Indians?"

"Vikings."

"Vikings? Like real burn-and-pillage vikings?"

"They were a Scandinavian clan that traveled over seven thousand kilometers and across the Bering Strait to get here." Taurus began walking as he spoke, and Jude followed to listen to the tale.

"They were a nomadic people, but when they saw this tree from a distance they ended up making camp all around it." As he spoke leather bound tents began popping up around them.

"They formed a village here, and for nearly one hundred years they lived around their great tree, Yggdrasil."

"The World Tree?" Jude asked as they stopped a moment. Before them and all around the scenery changed. Leather tents became wooden houses. The trees vanished and a long mead hall appeared. Guard towers built themselves as though my magic, connected by large wooden walls.

"Yes, they named it after their mythical world tree that ties together the nine realms."

"Fitting I guess," Jude shrugged as he pulled out his first notebook and began writing and sketching what he saw around him. "What made them so special that they had to be destroyed?"

Page 47

No sooner had the words left his lips than did a great wooden fortress arise from the ground. A veritable castle with turrets and levels upon levels. Great wooden spires extended off the turrets and it seemed like the castle might even challenge the tree for height.

"Now this, is unreal," Jude said, fervently sketching what he saw as Taurus lead him onward.

"Around the time Eric the Red's son, Lief, was discovering northeastern Canada, these people had complex government, a flourishing economy, agriculture, and education." Taurus walked directly to the front gates of the castle, and as he did the gates opened, not for him but for a group on horses. Still he and Jude passed through the castle gates quickly and into the main courtyard.

"They had a military," he continued, "since after all they were, how did you put it, pillagers?"

"These don't look like pillagers," Jude commented.

Taurus grinned.

"Nearly two hundred years after they left Europe and crossed the world on foot, their society was the most advanced North America had yet seen."

"Let me guess, until the Chaos?"

The two entered the main halls of the castle and made a sharp turn which lead down into the cellar. In the undercroft of the castle Jude noticed a group of twenty or so wearing robes and bowing before one man in a robe and a floppy leather hat, almost like an oversized fedora.

The people surrounding him were chanting something Jude did not understand, and the Hat Man was reading from a large tome of some sort that had a strange iron crest on its cover. Jude looked to Taurus for answers but the Zodiac merely stood silent with his arms crossed over his chest and a disgusted look painted on his face.

The Hat Man raised his voice and one arm as he chanted some incantation Jude had never heard. Suddenly one of the others surrounding him clutched at his own throat, fell to his side and appeared to be having a seizure. Jude watched carefully as Hat Man raised his fist again and another acolyte fell to their side, clutched their throat and also began seizing.

This happened again and again, until half the remaining worshippers were either shaking violently, or had stopped all together. Meanwhile, those that remained continued to bow up and down before the Hat Man as he read from the tome.

Then something changed.

Jude noticed the man's face had begun to shrivel, deep lines began to form in his cheeks and his eyes were sunken a bit. His lips curled and shrunk, allowing more of his teeth to show. He slammed the book shut and lowered his face to the ground, and mumbled something Jude couldn't hear.

"What's he saying? What's going on?" Jude asked, becoming increasingly concerned.

"There is evil in the hearts of men," Taurus finally answered. "Most hide it, some reveal it, and even some," he pointed at Hat Man, "nurture it."

Hat Man was now laughing, low and cruel but enough that his entire body shook with the laughter. Jude turned his eyes down and noticed the remaining men and women in robes were now also laying on the floor, apparently dead. Hat Man slowly raised his head and looked towards Jude. His eyes were gone, there only remained blackness through his squinted eyelids. The eyes hadn't so much as shrunk or faded, but it was though the sockets now reflected the darkness of space itself, with no beginning and no end.

Jude was horrified as he stared at the gaunt, eyeless face that looked in his direction. He reached out for Taurus' arm and gently tugged on his robe.

"Can we leave?"

"Worry not, he can neither see nor hear..."

"*Pro...phet...*" The Hat Man hissed.

The hair stood up on the back of Jude's neck and Taurus paused, now looking directly at the Hat Man, who merely chuckled.

"*I...see...you...*" he hissed again. Taurus thrust his elbow to the side.

"Take my arm!"

Jude obeyed without a second's notice.

The Hat Man continued laughing, louder and louder, until the undercroft literally shook with the sound of his voice.

"*Boom...*"

The walls around them, and the ceiling above them, exploded outwards in a flash of fire and light. Jude squinted to guard his eyes from the blast and clung tightly to Taurus' arm. Frantically Jude looked around at their situation.

The castle walls, doors, interior, furniture, everything was in the air and flying in slow motion outward. At the same time a crack had formed in the foundation between Hat Man's feet, and what looked to be roaches were pouring out of it by the dozens.

"Oh my god..." Jude said, as each roach transformed before his very eyes. They grew in shape and size as rapidly as they had emerged from the crevice. As they grew their legs took on the shape of a canine's, thick black hair sprouted from their necks to their hind quarters, and the snout of a wolf protruded from an otherwise head and face of a man.

The creatures Jude had come to know as Dark Ones didn't waste any time tearing into the homes and buildings surrounding the still flying castle. The Hat Man had turned his attention elsewhere and was now walking out of the newly formed crater with his tome in hand. He paused and turned to look directly at Taurus and Jude. What remained of his pale lips curled into an evil smile, baring now hundreds of sharp, jagged, yellow teeth.

"*See...you...soon...*" he hissed at them both.

"I thought you said they can't see me!? He definitely can see me!" Jude responded, now almost hiding behind Taurus.

"That...that has never happened before." Taurus said, more than a twinge of uncertainty in his voice. "Hold on."

The two then rose into the air, high into the air and back away from the great tree. Jude looked on as they hung in midair and watched the havoc beneath them. Homes and buildings burned, screams filled the evening air, and the fire spread to the boughs of the great tree itself.

All manner of birds that for centuries took up residence in the branches of Yggdrasil fled in a mass exodus. They cawed their displeasure as the flames climbed up the trunk to lick at their nests. A horrible circle of flames surrounded the tree, as wood and flesh alike burned.

"Look," Taurus pointed. From the sky, several objects like meteors, streaked down and landed throughout the Viking city. Again, like in Paris, Jude's eyes focused and zoomed like the vision of an eagle.

"Are those, people?" he asked.

"Indeed," Taurus answered. But his own eyes were searching the Chaos below for signs of the Hat Man.

"Those people are the ones you guys chose, aren't they? I don't want to say 'Chosen Ones' because that's super corny but... they're your Chos..."

"Stewards," Taurus corrected. "They are the Stewards of the Timeless. But yes, they are this age's defense against the Chaos."

"Did they succeed?"

"See for yourself."

Time then began to speed up, and the scene changed from night to day to night again. Branches burnt and filled the sky with black smoke, and then some fell and collapsed on the dead and living alike. The upper two thirds of the trunk both burned and rotted simultaneously, until the scene began to resemble the Devils Tower of modern day.

Jude watched as one of the Stewards leapt from the ground, and flew through the air, then landed atop the still burning lower portion of the tree. He couldn't see what was happening, but within moments the smoke, the flames, and the rot had all stopped. Then slowly, from the top down, the remaining stump transformed from wood, into grey stone.

Still clutching Taurus' arm Jude blinked and they were back along side the highway, half a kilometer from the Devils Tower, in modern day Wyoming.

"Come," Taurus said urgently. "We have much to do."

Chapter 5

"My sword is there?" asked Riku, as he looked on at the Devils Tower not far in the distance.

"You will find the sword of Achilles at the top of the rock formation." Sagittarius answered while looking around in all directions. "Something is off. I feel a presence here that should not be."

Riku ignored the warning, smiling up at the tower.

"It looks like a tree," he said.

"It was, long ago. It was attacked by flame and taint that threatened to burn and corrupt the entire nation."

"What stopped it?"

"The Warrior did." With that, Sagittarius gave his steed a slight kick and the horse took off fast up the hill towards the base of the Devils Tower. Riku did the same, urging his own horse to try and catch up.

It didn't take them long on horseback to reach the base of the tower, where grey rock had fallen off over the decades and formed a blanket all near the base. Riku looked around for a path upward.

"Do I have to climb it? I've never done rock climbing before. But I can do it if you need me to."

"No need," Sagittarius responded as he pulled his bow off the saddle.

"Oh no. You aren't doing that again are you?" The words barely left his mouth before an arrow went flying from the Zodiac's bow and Riku, screaming, followed. He landed on top of the tower and heaved in and out to catch his breath. As he looked up, he saw not seventy meters away, a tall skinny man in jeans and a long sleeve shirt, standing next to an even taller man in a hooded jacket with bull horns protruding from the front of his head.

"Who is that?," Riku asked. "Are they here for the sword? Should I fight them?" He dismounted his horse and made a face, jumping into a martial arts stance.

"I am Riku Yatsukura, the spring tiger, The Warrior! If you are my enemy, prepare to be vanquished!" He threw a series a kicks into the air, followed by random jumps, punches and spins. Truth be told, his athletic ability was impressive, even for his smaller stature.

Sagittarius watched him from the corner of his burning eyes, shook his head, and addressed Taurus.

"Greetings, brother. You have found the Prophet, I see."

"I have." Taurus replied. "And you, The Warrior."

Sagittarius nodded and waved a hand towards Riku, who still kicked and spun in his demonstration. "The Warrior has come for the sword. But why are you here? Why bring The Prophet?"

Riku stopped his kicking.

"The Prophet? You're one of us?"

"My name is Jude. Taurus calls me The Prophet. You can call me Jude." Jude replied.

"No way! And you speak Japanese as well! But you look American?"

Jude cocked his head in confusion and looked to Taurus for an explanation.

"You each speak your own language, but you are Stewards now, and thus must be able to communicate with one another. Each hears and understands in his own language, even while speaking to one another in a language foreign to them." Then he addressed Sagittarius.

"We would not be here, normally. I have shown The Prophet the fall of the Kingdom of Himinn, but there was an anomaly in the past I have not seen before. Tell me, what of our brothers and sisters?"

Sagittarius rode closer to Jude and Taurus, and Riku followed, leaving his horse where it was.

"Aries has located The Healer. The other Stewards have not been gathered."

"What of Aquarius?" Taurus prodded.

"He observes, but does not seek a Steward."

"And the Twins?"

"I have not had contact with the Twins, or Scorpio or Cancer."

"Curious," Taurus looked about as he spoke. "This is unusual."

"Look there!" Riku shouted. Everyone turned to see a dark black sludge crawling up the side of the tower and over the edge. It was slick and oily, but also gave off the very powerful scent of burning flesh, so much it made Jude gag. It grew into the shape of a person, and in moments had transformed into a man wearing a dirty black duster, pants, boots, and a long-brimmed black fedora.

"*Welcome...back.*" Hat Man hissed as he looked up from under his brim. His face was gaunt and shriveled, the eyelids squinted but left enough room for the emptiness that would have been where the eyeballs were, except there weren't any. His many jagged yellow teeth shone with his crooked smile.

"Oh my god, it's him." Jude slapped Taurus on the arm. "That was what, a thousand years ago? How can this be possible?"

"How many times...have we seen each other...Zodiac? Hmmmm? Seven? Eight?" Hat Man hissed as he took steps closer to the group.

"You have never seen me, monster." Taurus replied.

"I have...always seen you...but never had the pleasure...of seeing your...protege."

"Is this who I need to fight?" asked Riku. "Do you have the sword of Achilles, demon!?" he demanded. Hat Man laughed.

"The sword of Achilles? What do...you teach these children? There is no...sword here, boy. You have been fooled...lied to...by cosmic beings intent on...status quo."

"Silence your tongue!" Sagittarius barked. His eyes shot brighter as the fire within them flared. "We have come to destroy you and your ilk!"

"Age after...age. You have never destroyed my master. You...have lost. Every. Single. Time," he hissed and choked and laughed, standing up straighter he seemed to even grow a bit.

"I saw you, you're just a man." Jude said.

"Was, boy. Was a man. You saw the ritual, yes? Immortality feeds on...life. My master feeds...on death."

From all around them, claws reached over the edges of the tower as Dark Ones began climbing up onto the plateau. They moaned, snarled, and growled, encircling the four and drawing closer.

"Now...die." Hat Man hissed loudly, his voice seemed to echo from all around them.

"Get behind me!" both Zodiac shouted in unison. Jude and Riku obeyed, coming close together with the Zodiac on either outside edge.

Sagittarius swiftly grabbed his bow from the saddle, and in an instant had an arrow nocked. His normally plain helmet grew a wide, brass "U" shape on the forehead that, once complete, ignited with fire the same color as his eyes.

Taurus flung his hood over his head as it changed color into a dark, deep red. Armor like molten gold formed around his arms, waist, and legs. A golden helmet formed around his head, leaving only a small slit down the front and across the eyes. New horns, covered in gold, grew into a more elaborate shape from the sides of the helmet. Jude watched in amazement while Taurus held out his arm and the remaining gold formed into an elegant and massive lance.

The Dark Ones waited no more, and charged the small group. The first leapt towards Riku and instantly flew back and over the edge of the tower as it was impaled with an arrow. With a loud grunt, Taurus charged forward, head slightly bowed, fittingly, and skewered two of the beasts on his lance. He hurled the carcasses at Hat Man, who laughed and stepped aside.

The scene became a dizzying whirlwind for Jude and Riku to watch. Taurus fought and flowed, spun and turned not unlike a bucking bull. Meanwhile, Sagittarius rode his horse and shot arrow after arrow, directing his steed with not so much as a single kick. Surely anyone observing would say that horse and rider were one.

"Taurus! The ground!" Sagittarius shouted.

Taurus struck his lance into a Dark One, and pinned it to the ground then knelt and pounded the dirt once with his free fist. A crack ran from his fist toward the center of the tower and stopped. Then he stood up, flung the beast off, and charged another.

"What do you and I do? Do we fight? Do you have a weapon?" Riku asked Jude, somewhat panicking.

"I have notebooks and pens," Jude replied. "I don't think we can help."

Jude looked over to Hat Man, and noticed he was walking in their direction.

"Uh, maybe, run!?" Jude suggested, grabbing Riku by the arm they ran in the opposite direction.

"Warrior! The center!" Sagittarius yelled, his horse trampling the enemy underfoot.

Riku turned his attention to the center of the tower, as Taurus knelt on the other end and pounded a fist into the ground again. Another crack appeared and ran to the center until more rocks broke free.

"Look! Can you see that?" He spun Jude around and pointed towards the center. Jude squinted his eyes, the eagle vision returned, and he could see very clearly what appeared to be the pommel of a sword in the rock where Taurus can ruptured the tower.

"Oh, you've got to be kidding me!" Jude looked up, noticing Hat Man closing the distance between them, and heading right toward the center itself, though Jude couldn't tell if he saw what was there.

"Come on! We've got to hurry!" Jude pulled Riku, and the two ran towards Hat Man.

"*Yessss....come to your deaths!*" he hissed.

Sagittarius watched from the corner of his eye as the two stewards ran towards their foe. He loosed another arrow, striking and blowing back a Dark One that nearly had it's jaws on Jude's shoulder. Then another that swung a clawed hand at Riku.

The pair reached the center and saw the pommel and half the handle of a sword buried into the rock. Riku grabbed it and tried pulling, but it wouldn't budge.

"I can't get it out!" he cried, looking up at Hat Man only a few meters away.

"Taurus!" Jude shouted. "He can't pull it out!"

Taurus pounded a fist into the dirt from another angle. Another crack.

More rock broke and the hilt became visible.

"Past, present, future! You see it, Prophet! Use it!" Taurus shouted.

Jude looked frantically at the battle around them. More and more Dark Ones were climbing over the edges and attacking the Zodiac. Hat Man was almost upon them. The sword could be no more than wiggled, but it was coming loose. He closed his eyes tight to think.

"Keep trying! I'm going to buy you a little more time." Riku looked into Jude's eyes, unsure of what to say as the latter stood up and marched towards Hat Man. Riku turned his attention back to the sword and continued to tug on the handle.

Jude couldn't breathe. A week ago he was an introverted, mid-30s, single man living in a small apartment in Southern California. He worked his job, paid his bills, watched TV and played video games. On the weekend he got together with a few guys, and one girl he had been crushing on, to play Dungeons & Dragons and drink soda.

Now he stood on top of a national monument, surrounded by demonic man-beasts, charging down a one thousand year old necromancer, armed with paper and pens.

"Come on, Jude," he whispered to himself. "Roll a twenty."

He came face to face with Hat Man, who was much taller up close than at a distance. Jude grabbed him by the elbows, noticing that there wasn't much to this creature. Hat Man returned the sentiment, grabbing Jude by the triceps. His grip was powerful, beguiling his appearance.

"*Come to die?*" He hissed. Jude turned away, his breath was atrocious.

"Geez man…no not really." Jude responded.

"*A pity. Last words?*"

"Yeah, one." Jude smiled, while Hat Man cocked his head. "Boom."

Off to the side, Taurus raised both hands into the air, his lance on the ground, Dark Ones leaping towards him. He smashed his fists into the dirt, causing the tower itself to shake. Another crack shot down from Taurus to the center where rock and dust exploded.

Jude heaved as hard as he could and pulled Hat Man to the side to shield himself from the exploding rock.

Hat Man laughed.

"*A fool's errand…I'm afraid.*" He opened his mouth wide. Jude saw fear, darkness, evil, an emptiness that could never be filled if it consumed entire galaxies. He felt himself being pulled into that gaping mouth. No, not himself, his *soul*.

Suddenly Hat Man shrieked. Jude looked down and saw a double edged blade protruding from Hat Man's stomach.

"I got you, demon!" Riku shouted.

Hat Man shrieked again, and the Dark Ones fled as quickly as they had arrived. Hat Man looked down into Jude's eyes. Words, unspoken filled Jude's mind.

Then he exploded into a million flies, which swarmed Riku momentarily, and then took off to the east. Stunned and stuttering, Jude fell to his knees and stared at the rocky floor.

"I did it!" Riku yelled. "Woohoo! I killed the demon!"

Sagittarius paused a moment, then trotted over to survey the aftermath.

"He is not dead," the Zodiac said. "Only harmed. The two of you did well."

Taurus walked over as well, the armor melted away and his jacket returned to normal. He approached Jude, who slowly looked up at him.

"Are you harmed, Prophet?" he asked. Jude, still shocked from the jarring experience, slowly nodded.

"I know where they're attacking next," he choked out.

Chapter 6

Samantha was amazed at the absolute grandeur of The Grand Egyptian Museum. She had never been to Africa before, or any other country for that matter. She rarely left Brooklyn when she wasn't working. But here she was, standing before the brand new museum, and if the outward appearance wasn't amazing enough, she couldn't begin to guess what was inside.

As she stepped into the entrance, she was greeted by the red granite statue of Ramesses II, towering over her at eleven meters high. Her jaw dropped and she almost walked into a velvet rope from her lack of attention.

"It's okay, we expect that reaction from people," came a voice with a thick accent from in front of Samantha. She looked down, shocked, and saw a Middle Eastern woman in a long dress and head scarf, smiling back at her.

"Oh, I'm so sorry, I didn't see you there." Samantha apologized.

"It's okay. I am happy you like it," she held out a hand. "I am Dr. Yasmine Saliba. I am the curator here at the Grand Egyptian Museum. I was told you were coming."

"You were?" Samantha was surprised. "By who?"

"By her," Dr. Saliba pointed to Samantha's right side, where Aries stood over both women. Samantha looked up, and then back at Dr. Saliba with wide eyes.

"You can *see* her?"

Dr. Saliba laughed. "Of course I can. But I think not everybody could, hmmm? If you will please follow me, I believe I know what you are looking for."

Samantha looked up to Aries for direction, but the Zodiac merely nodded her approval and the three women headed down the long halls of the museum.

"We have just over one hundred thousand Egyptian artifacts on display," Dr. Saliba spoke as they walked, "including over three thousand treasures of King Tutankhamen's tomb, sarcophagi from within each of the pyramids, as well as from dozens of surrounding tombs." She held out a hand gesturing for Samantha to go ahead into an elevator. Dr. Saliba followed, while Aries stood outside as the elevator doors closed.

As they started down, she turned to Samantha and gently touched her arm.

"What is it like? To converse with the Timeless one. You must be so excited and nervous, hmm?"

Samantha forced an uneasy smile.

"Yes, I guess. It's kind of surreal and confusing to be honest. I've seen a lot of things in my job, but nothing like this."

"I can imagine! You have no idea how long I have hoped to see this in my lifetime!"

Samantha looked at the doctor and furrowed her eyebrows.

"What do you mean? You know about all this?"

"You are here because of the stone, yes?" Samantha nearly fell over.

"So you do know about all this?"

"Oh yes! There are records everywhere. I cannot wait to show you…"

The elevator doors opened and there stood Aries, waiting for them both.

"Oh! Oh my goodness, you surprised me!" laughed Dr. Saliba. Giggling, she lead Samantha down another series of halls, through locked doors, more halls, and even to a dead end that didn't seem to have door at all.

Dr. Saliba leaned in close to one of the small pyramid designs that dotted the entire wall. A red light passed over her open eyes, and the wall itself begin to open for her. With a big smile on her face, she entered and waved for Samantha to follow.

"You guys love your security," Samantha commented.

"The artifacts you see in the museum, however great, are only half of what we actually store here. With it's completion, the Grand Egyptian now contains artifacts from around the world, with a larger collection than the Vatican vaults."

She stopped at a large, black, steel box, one of many in the room with both numbers and Arabic written on it. She passed a key fob over the box, and it responded with beeps and a small flashing light before a mechanical clicking sound and the middle drawer slid open.

"Here it is," Dr. Saliba announced with a great smile, offering Samantha to take a look. "The armband of Cleopatra."

Samantha gazed down at the beautiful crescent piece of jewelry, comprised completely of gold with tiny rubies encrusted in it. She looked up at Aries who stood by silently, and for the first time saw a striking resemblance in the design and color scheme to the armor Aries wore.

"You can't ask me to take this," Samantha objected.

"Why not? It is meant for you. We do not know when the last Healer wore this, but we do know you will be needing it now." Dr. Saliba pushed back the glass covering and picked up the armband, twisting it to show Samantha the detail.

"It was recorded, this band was a gift to Cleopatra from Marc Antony himself when he visited her in Alexandria. See here?" She pointed at engravings on the side which read 'SPQR'. "With this engraving, Cleopatra was treated as a Roman citizen, even as she ruled Egypt."

Dr. Saliba gently handed it to Samantha who took it as though handling a newborn baby. She carefully looked at the armband and shook her head.

"I don't understand. It's just a piece of jewelry. How can this heal people?"

"The Prophet writes that 'through the armband, The Healer cleansed the sick. The taint had no effect on those she touched'. But as for how it works, I am afraid that is your secret."

"The Prophet? The Healer? So there's been others then?"

"Yes," Dr. Saliba closed the drawer. "We know of only two. And only through the records of The Prophet do we know of those, though there may have been more. The records were…badly preserved."

Samantha looked up to Aries, who had been silent all this time. She held up the armband for Aries to see.

"Well, what do you think?" she asked.

"You are The Healer," she said softly. Dr. Saliba gasped and covered her mouth.

"The voice of an angel," the doctor whispered, enamored.

Aries continued.

"This belongs to you, Samantha. If you believe in what I've told you, you may heal millions. If not, millions will suffer, and their rot will plague this world."

"Geez, no pressure right?" Samantha sighed heavily as she looked at the armband. She shook her head and closed her eyes, trying to muster the will and the belief.

Suddenly before her eyes, she saw the Hispanic man from just a day ago. She could feel his body under her hands as she tried to get his heart beating again. She felt the heat, strange and unfamiliar, coursing under her and how time itself seemed to slow. She felt his very life trying to return to his body, like she was commanding his soul back to where it belonged. She could feel his soul.

Aries smirked, while Dr. Saliba stared on with wide eyes. The rubies in the armband were sparkling and glowing as Samantha held it in her hands and focused on her lost patient. Dr. Saliba fought to keep from gasping, but she relented, almost in tears.

Samantha opened her eyes at the sound, drawn out of her trance, and noticed the glowing rubies. She jumped and let go of the piece, letting it fall and bounce on the floor. Stunned, Samantha covered her own mouth, surprised at her own reaction. Her fists tightened and she knelt to grab the armband again, holding it tight this time.

The rubies shone even brighter than before, drawing a shriek of excitement from Dr. Saliba. Samantha grinned and fixed the band on her upper arm, it fit nicely. She held out a hand, as her eyes glowed to match the rubies.

"Dr. Saliba, thank you so much. I think I have work to get to."

Riku may as well have been as tall as Taurus or Sagittarius the way he rode his horse after battle. With the Sword of Achilles fastened on his back, which may have also helped his upright posture, he wore the look of a victorious conquerer. His eyes stared straight down at the horizon before them, as all four traveled in a group, for now, for safety given the uncertainty of the attack by Hat Man.

Jude on the other hand, was lost in his own thoughts, or the thoughts implanted by his adversary, and only looked up to Riku now and then with a mild sense of judgement. Jude was many years his senior, and had been the first to confront Hat Man head on, thus giving Riku time to try and pry the sword from the stone, as it were. In his eyes, Riku did very little to assist at all in that last battle.

But he would let Riku have his moment of victory, for now, while his mind raced towards other things. Darker things.

"What did you see?" Taurus asked, snapping Jude out of his train of thoughts.

"Sorry, what?"

"I have stewarded prophets before you, though my duty has fallen elsewhere, and I recognize that look you wear."

"Elsewhere?" Jude was desperate to change the subject. "Like other stewards? Which ones? Anyone noteworthy? Riku said Sagittarius trained Achilles…"

"He did. Achilles was a great Warrior, beyond compare and second to none," Taurus gave a wry smile, "except maybe Heracles."

Jude flashed a look at him. And could swear he heard Sagittarius sigh.

"Hercules? The Greek myth. Come on, everybody knows that's just a legend."

"Indeed, he was a legend. I was tasked with his training, although his 'twelve labors' have been romanticized a bit." Taurus suddenly threw his head back and let out a loud and hearty laugh. "Sagittarius! Do you remember when I convinced Leo to wrestle with Heracles?!"

Sagittarius shook his head.

"Every age you reminisce about that. I'd think Leo would sooner have you forget it," he said.

"Leo was so certain no human could ever beat him, so he agreed to the challenge. The look on his face when Heracles threw him to the ground and pinned his arm behind his back!" Taurus roared with laughter again. This time, Sagittarius let out a little chuckle as well.

"Do you mean the Nemean Lion? Leo was the Nemean Lion Hercules had to slay?" Jude stopped walking, pretended to be engaged in the story, and while it was entertaining and odd to see the very serious Zodiac laughing, he was glad for the distraction.

"The slaying part was a bit exaggerated. Leo eventually freed himself, and tossed Heracles into a field..."

"A mere ten seconds later," Sagittarius added.

"But for his effort, Leo gave him the Golden Fleece, a cloak no blade could ever penetrate. No claw either, not even from a Dark One."

Riku perked up at hearing this.

"Is that the next artifact for The Warrior?"

"The Sword will suit you well enough," Sagittarius said sternly. "Besides, with that recent attack I fear time may be against us."

"Which reminds me," Taurus said, turning to Jude. "What did you see?"

Jude was happy for the brief distraction and had hoped it got the Zodiac off the topic. But apparently his misdirection wasn't as well orchestrated as he thought.

"You know, don't you?" he said softly.

"I am not The Prophet. I know what I must know, and nothing beyond that. It is you that was chosen to be Keeper of the Tomes." Taurus leaned down a bit, pressing into Jude's bubble. Jude raised an eyebrow.

"Tell me, why did you purchase pens and notebooks?" Taurus pressed.

Jude shrugged. "I don't know. I figured I'd need to write some stuff down."

"Exactly. Every Prophet of every age has kept tomes, written records of what has been, what is, and what will be."

"You can see the future?" Riku interrupted. Jude shook his head.

"No. Well, I don't know. Right after you stabbed…that thing…I caught a glimpse of something like a movie playing out in my head."

"Right. Then you said you know where the enemy is striking next. But you have been silent since then." Riku leaned over the neck of his horse in order to speak softer.

"Listen, I may be be a mighty warrior, but I am only a young man as well."

"I'm at least fifteen years older than you…" Jude scoffed.

"Still. If we are to be a team, promise me something. That we will both agree to do our best to save everyone." At this Riku held out a hand.

Jude looked up at the short teenager atop his brown horse. His honest smile and smooth skin made him look even younger than he was. But it was at the least an honest smile. Here was a man, albeit young, who truly believed and hung on every word the Zodiac had said. And one who truly believed that with their guidance he could make a real difference in whatever chaos was coming.

Jude sighed and took Riku's hand.

"Ok. Let's wing this thing."

"Excellent! So where are we headed, partner?" Riku sat back up in his saddle, excited to keep moving.

"There's something in Africa, a lot of sick people. Trees dying and water being polluted and some woman trying to make it all better. But she doesn't. She's dying too, just, slower than everyone else..." Jude trailed off after this, he eyes fixed on a spot on the ground, but seeing so much more.

Taurus looked to Sagittarius with a frown on his face.

"The stone has been found," he said.

"And The Healer as well," Sagittarius replied.

"No, not a stone," Jude muttered, almost as if now caught in a trance. "It's not a stone. It's a diamond."

"A diamond that makes people sick? That doesn't sound right." Riku shifted in his saddle.

"The diamond was a gift to Pharaoh, stolen by the king of another country. The stone itself was cursed to poison all who touch it." Taurus turned back to Jude, "but I have not yet shown you that. Your ability is coming fast."

"He has seen what is to come, and The Healer is in danger. I will take The Warrior and meet with Aries. She was
Page 73

charged with finding The Healer." Sagittarius said as he turned his horse to a different direction and drew his bow from the saddle.

"And I will take The Prophet…"

"Jude."

"…to the next age he must witness. The enemy is moving fast. We must match his pace."

Sagittarius nodded in agreement and loosed an arrow into the open air. Before Riku could open his mouth to say goodbye, or protest, they were both gone and only Taurus and Jude were left standing on the road.

———

Paris could not be kept a secret for long. Even with governments of multiple countries flagging and removing user submitted videos of the disaster and horror taking place, those videos simply were uploaded hours later to different web sites. The mass panic country leaders had hoped to prevent was on the verge of eruption.

Soon, web sites rose and fell declaring the attack a massive government conspiracy. Rumors swirled about an alien invasion from another planet that threatened humanity's existence. Religious groups gathered in the streets of every major capital demanding that something be done about this unprecedented event. Even more groups signaled the end of days. They weren't wrong.

Within days, the United Nations sent reconnaissance fighters and helicopters into the area to assess the situation, but those were swatted out of the sky by high jumping Dark

Ones and their deadly claws. Next thermal imaging was brought into play by high orbiting satellites, but only the wounded survivors could be seen. It was as though the Dark Ones gave off no heat, no thermal footprint at all. As though the very fabric of their being was, true to their name, darkness.

By Day 8, boots on the ground entered the remains of Paris with live-streaming body cams attached to each soldier. The world's leaders got to watch in real time as their elite were ripped to pieces by the vicious beasts that now inhabited the City of Light. Ten days after the initial onslaught, the nuclear option was put on the table, only to be derided by the leaders of Europe.

While the world grew more and more desperate for a solution, the worst had not yet even been unleashed. It was at the Arch de Triumph, or what was left of it, that the Dark Ones assembled the pieces of their long since destroyed general, the Wicked Man. His limbs, torso, and everything else had been exhumed from the catacombs beneath Paris and laid together on the cobblestone beneath the Arch itself.

A dozen Dark Ones circled the body and bowed, putting their heads to the stone, as a fedora-wearing figure stepped into the circle. Hat Man smiled his jagged-tooth grin as he pulled the ancient tome of the Viking city from his duster and opened to bookmarked pages.

As he had over one thousand years ago, he began reading from the tome, and one by one the surrounding dark servants fell to the ground writhing and moaning in pain. And one by one, the writhing stopped as the life was drained into the bones of the Wicked Man.

Hat Man continued his incantations as he backed out of the circle until the last Dark One was laying dead at his feet. He shut the tome with a snap and wheezed with excitement.

Page 75

"Arise...my general." He hissed.

The dead bodies in the circle all at once turned to blackened dust and ash, and swarmed over the bones. The ash formed robes and a hood and lifted the skeleton, nearly three meters in height, to it's feet. The hood covered over the eyes but the feet stood and the skeletal arms grew black, rotting flesh. The corpse let out a cry that echoed and elicited howls throughout the burnt city.

"You have brought me back, Rezzek," the Wicked Man's voice was low, but reverberated like a nightmare.

"I am...ready to serve...once more."

"I smell the dead. What city have you taken?"

"We began the assault...on the home...of the Merovingians." Hat Man, called Rezzek, bowed low and smiled.

"Good work, servant. We shall begin here then. The Master wants all of them, every enlightened kingdom, thrown into the Chaos." Wicked Man growled.

He peered around the city at the destruction and death everywhere and chuckled deep and low, but nevertheless loud enough to be heard for a distance.

"Their armies can do nothing, I see. There is little resistance?"

"Little...however," Rezzek bowed even lower. *"The Zodiac have appeared. Their warrior...has the sword. Their prophet...has not discovered his power...yet."*

Wicked Man shot a look at Rezzek, and even though it was through empty eye sockets filled with the same darkness in his own, the look nearly knocked Rezzek over.

"The Master's plan must not be disturbed. My punishment was severe for my failure ages ago. Yours will be legendary. Do not face the Stewards until..."

Wicked Man's focus suddenly turned to Rezzek's torso as noticed something near his belly. A cut, no a burn, in the cloth that was also oozing a black liquid.

"What weapon ran you through?" he demanded.

Rezzek bowed even lower, attempting to cover the cut. Wicked Man raised his palm and Rezzek was forced to stand up straight, even lifted off his feet and floated in midair before the skeletal gaze.

"Your *general* asked a question of you," Wicked Man growled, his voice boomed and shook the pavement nearby.

"*The Sword of...Achilles, master.*" Rezzek squirmed and whimpered out.

"So you faced them already?"

"*I sensed the Prophet...I did not see the warrior...he did not have the weapon. He retrieved it...at...*"

"Yggdrasil. So they are moving quickly." Wicked Man dropped his hand and Rezzek fell to his feet. "There has not been an age they have succeeded in saving in quite some time. We cannot allow them to succeed now. Go to the stone and see that the taint is spread. I will marshal our forces here and await the Master."

"*He is coming...here?*"

"Yes. Apollyon wishes to lay waste to this age himself."

Without another word the Wicked Man lifted off from the stone as light as a feather in the breeze and headed for the center of the city. Rezzek watched his risen master leave and unconsciously moved a hand over the rotting puncture wound in his abdomen.

His body burst into thousands of flies and spun in a vortex as they sped off in the opposite direction towards the southern horizon.

Page 77

Chapter 7

♈

Within moments of stepping out of the Grand Egyptian Museum, Samantha and Aries were both whisked away and soon stood on the bank of Lake Victoria, near the border of Kenya and Uganda. Samantha staggered a bit from the sudden displacement, and closed her eyes tight to regain her footing.

"Where are we now?" she asked as she rubbed her forehead.

"Sio," Aries answered. "In Africa. I'm afraid we're running behind, however."

Aries pointed as Samantha looked up to see a lake barge pulling up to the shore fifty meters away from them. The men on the barge were cheering, and a large crowd had gathered on the bank to greet them.

"Is that it? Is that the stone?" Samantha squinted, trying to focus.

"It is," Aries nodded.

The men jumped off the barge into the waist-deep water and together hoisted off a large, near colorless, rough diamond. The crowd on the shore cheered, and Samantha suddenly noticed the dozen men nearby in fatigues carrying very large rifles. She turned to Aries in shock.

"Is that a diamond?!"

"It is," Aries answered, just as coolly.

"You said it was a stone. That's not a stone, that's a big ass diamond!" Though Samantha shouted, no one nearby paid her any mind, they were too busy looking at the historical rock.

"A diamond is a stone. It may be precious here, but when measured against eternity it's just another rock." Samantha's jaw hit the floor as she stared at Aries.

"How did a diamond that big not get noticed before? That's easily the size of a child! I can see it clearly from here, it's huge. It has to weigh…"

"Forty kilograms."

"Forty kilograms?! I don't even know how many carats that is!"

"Two hundred thousand carats, by your measurements."

Samantha collapsed to her knees in the mud.

"You can't be serious," she murmured. "You do realize that no one will ever, ever, let me anywhere near that thing, right? Look at those armed guards! They see me walking in their direction and they'll kill me on sight."

Her eyes gazed over passed the bank, and she noticed a large temporary tent set up. Then she saw the cars, dozens of cars parked in the area and just before asking where the media coverage was, she noticed the news vans lined up in the distance with names written in a dozen languages. But no one except the small crowd, which turned out to be workers as she saw, and the dozen men with rifles were anywhere actually near the massive rock.

"I still don't get it," she muttered. "No one ever saw it there?"

"No one ever looked. It has been hidden in mud and muck for centuries, but now the one who seeks to end your world has revealed the location of the stone."

"Diamond," Samantha corrected.

"The stone is tainted with evil that poisons any who touch it. You can heal the taint so long as you wear the Armband of Cleopatra. Keep a sharp eye, for all who have already handled it are doomed for death. They…"

Aries froze and stopped mid sentence. She stared straight ahead unblinking, unmoving.

"Aries?" Samantha nudged her. "Aries are you ok?"

"They shouldn't be here," she said, in a tone very different from moments before.

"Who shouldn't? Hey snap out of it you're scaring me." Samantha tried to shake her, but the Zodiac would not budge. It was like trying to shake a statue.

"You are in danger, Healer. How could I have missed this?"

From across the lake there came a swirling mass of flies, headed in their direction. Samantha noticed it first, or she thought she did, and she pointed out a hand towards the bugs.

"Okay, now that doesn't look natural."

"He cannot be here, not yet." Aries broke her statue-like mode and turned to face the swarm coming over the lake. The flies swirled and came to rest near the bank, where they coalesced and took solid form. Rezzek, the Hat Man, stood before Aries and Samantha and smiled.

"*Zodiac…it's always…a pleasure.*"

"What business do you have here, creature?!" Aries demanded. Samantha took a step backwards, a bit more frightened at Aries' change in demeanor than this new gaunt figure that appeared.

"*Where are your…manners, Timeless One? I did miss you so…*" Rezzek chuckled as he spoke, like the whole thing was a great joke to him.

"My name is Aries, and I have no manners for you."

"Aries, we are on...first name terms again...well that changes things."

"Aries, what is he talking about?" Samantha asked, backing a little further away.

"Did you tell her? About me? About us?"

"Silence, creature!" Aries shouted, as her hand crossed her hip and gripped the handle of a gold and jewel encrusted dagger that Samantha swore wasn't there before.

"Come Zodiac, let's reason...let's talk...let's remi-nisce..."

"I said, you will call me Aries," her voice resounded on itself as though echoing across the lake and back one hundred times. Samantha looked and saw black smoke coming from under Rezzek's duster. It gathered behind him, growing and wiggling, it moved like it was alive.

"Aries..." Samantha warned.

The smoke grew larger, taking the shape of a human skull, but twisted and tormented almost as though it was trying to scream. It grew larger, twice it's original size, then grew again, until the skull was as large as the Hat Man himself.

"Aries...Aries...shall I whisper it for you...as I con-sume your steward?" Rezzek grinned his toothy smile and Samantha began to get light headed.

"No," Aries said flatly, "but you may scream it...as you burn!"

The smoke skull opened it's wide mouth, and Samantha felt like a part of her was being drawn into it. She collapsed to her knees and placed shaky hands in the mud. Though her body didn't move, she dug her hands into the mud to avoid being sucked in.

But then Aries acted.

The Zodiac drew the golden dagger from her belt, and arched it across the sky. The blade appeared to hit nothing, but then a tear in midair ripped open before her. The tear opened wide in a matter of milliseconds, and fire burst out from it. Samantha watched in awe as the giant head of a ram, flaming bright as the sun, raised up and took aim at Rezzek. It's eyes blazed blue, it's horns a dazzling white and red that danced over the flames, and the rest of it orange and bright. The ram lowered it's head and charged forward.

Rezzek looked upwards, his smile gone, his jaw slack, as the ram crashed down on him and the smoking skull.

"*Aaaarrrrriiiieeeessss*!!!"

The water behind the Hat Man hissed and sizzled, steam shot up in all directions as the ram went head first into the lake itself. Samantha's eyes were wide and her mouth hung open as she watched the creature, and his torment, disappear. She gazed down and noticed a few dozen flies, smoking and circling as if they themselves were in a daze. They rose up and quickly darted off over the lake.

"What…was that?!" Samantha stood to her feet, mud covered most of her arms and pants. She took in long, hard breaths as her eyes darted from the lake to Aries and back.

"A servant of the Chaotic One," Aries said, her voice returned to the serene calm from before. "He's gone now, and should no longer bother you or your mission."

"But he knew you. Was he some kind of demon or monster or what? And you killed him right? And how did he know we would be here?"

Aries turned from the lake, her head down and eyes closed. When she reopened them there was a deep sapphire-blue glow emitting from them. Samantha stopped cold with her questions and felt a peace returning to her. She took a deep breath and the worries of the attack melted away, her mind focused on the task at hand: saving lives.

"He is of no consequence. Your target has moved, and is now in the presence of many people. If you wish to save them and the lives of everyone they will come into contact with, we must hurry."

Suddenly an arrow whistled into the area right nearby where they stood. It was caught midair by a large samurai sitting atop an equally impressive black steed. Both Aries and Samantha turned to look at this newcomer, but neither felt alarmed by his appearance.

"Greetings, sister," Sagittarius nodded to Aries. "And greetings to you, Healer. I am Sagittarius, the Archer. And this," he held a hand out to his side, and with a loud pop and a small burst of mist, a young Japanese man appeared, also on a horse, albeit one much smaller than the former's.

"This is The Warrior." Sagittarius announced.

"Ugh...I am not getting used to that," Riku leaned over the neck of his horse, who was staggering a bit as well. He straightened up and swallowed his heart and lungs back into place and turned his eyes to Samantha.

"Very nice to meet you. I'm Riku Yatsukura. The Warrior," he smiled and gave a customary bow.

"The Warrior huh?" Samantha gave him a quick look. "I'm Samantha, The Healer."

"Ohhh, you're the one Jude said was dying!" Riku covered his mouth.

"What?!" Samantha marched towards him. "Who said I was dying?"

"Sagittarius, what is the meaning of this?" Aries moved towards the other Zodiac, as Samantha advanced on Riku.

Page 83

"The Prophet has seen the stone. He has seen The Healer curing people, but his vision included her affected by the taint." Sagittarius turned a stern eye to Samantha. "Have you been infected?"

Aries spun on her heels and pressed her hands against both Samantha's collarbone and back simultaneously.

"She is clean," she announced.

"Good. We have come to help her stay that way," Sagittarius removed his helmet and mask, and Samantha stole a glance at his red, flaming eyes.

"So there's a prophet, too? And a warrior, and I'm a healer. Who else is there?" Samantha looked back to Riku. "And you have a sword, I see. A gift?" She pointed to the armband on her right bicep.

"Mmhmm," Riku nodded. "There are more, yes?" he asked of the Zodiac.

"As I told you before, Healer, there are twelve in all. But time is running short. The tent." Aries pointed towards the tent where the sounds of much revelry could be heard.

Samantha's eyes widened, and she spun towards the tent and began to run, then stopped and came back for Riku.

"If you're here to help, get off your horse and come with me."

"Lead the way!" Riku quickly dismounted, his sword on his back, and the two raced towards the tent. The two Zodiac watched while Aries breathed a heavy sigh.

"What troubles you, sister?" asked Sagittarius.

"Rezzek was here," she said, solemnly.

"He attacked us at Yggdrasil. The Warrior stabbed him with the Sword of Achilles, but he fled before he was finished."

"He attempted to consume The Healer. I burnt him, but I could not kill him."

"You could not have even if you had wanted to," Sagittarius reached down and touched her on the shoulder. "Neither life nor death, can we grant to humans. You know this."

"I do. I did not want to kill him. Part of him is still in there." Aries reached up and placed her hand on Sagittarius'.

"He is beyond our help. What was human is only rotted flesh. His soul belongs to his dark master."

"I failed him," she said, her voice barely audible.

"We have all failed."

"Tell me, do you think I will become like Aquarius?" Aries looked up at Sagittarius with sad, torn eyes.

"Never! You have not abandoned your charge! Look and see! The Healer runs into danger to carry out her tasks. You have done well in this age, and every age before!"

Aries looked back towards the tent just as Samantha and Riku slipped around the corner.

"Perhaps this time, it will be enough."

Riku was both excited and terrified to have a woman, a red-headed, American woman, holding his hand so tightly. Even if it was only to lead him into certain trouble and potential death. But in his mind, that was just a normal thing for a woman to do.

He felt as though his skin was too many shades of red but it appeared Samantha didn't notice. Or if she noticed, she didn't care. He was doing his best to summon his strict Bushido spirit and training and focus for the task at hand.

Task at hand. Task at hand. At hand. Hand. She's holding my hand! Her hand…

Page 85

His thoughts were everywhere except where he wanted them to be. No wonder his grandfather had told so many stories of his grandmother and called her a "wild woman". But this woman was a stranger, even if their fates had been entwined by the Timeless Zodiac of the stars.

Our fates, written in the stars before there was Time.

Riku shook his head violently in attempt to clear his mind, and in doing so almost ran into the corner post of the large tent as Samantha stopped cold.

"Shhhh, hold on. There's an entrance, but there are armed guards," she whispered.

"Let me take a look," Riku released her hand, reluctantly, and peeked around the corner of the tent. Several very large African men, dressed in fatigues, and carrying assault rifles, each with a pistol on his hip as well, stood watch. They guarded what looked to be the only entrance to the tent. Inside was chatter and laughing, voices of different languages carrying on excitedly.

"What are we going to do?" Samantha asked.

"What do you need to do? Get in there?" Riku pulled back.

"I don't know. I only know everyone who touches that diamond will get sick, and spread it to everyone else they touch."

"It's a diamond?"

"We need to get in there! But I don't want to get shot!" Samantha was whispering as loud as she could without yelling. Riku nodded his understanding and drew his sword. He held it out in front of him with both hands barely fitting on the hand-and-a-half handle.

He hadn't really taken the time to examine the sword before, but it was a magnificent piece of work. It was a Xiphos style of sword with a handle made of bronze. It had a square design to it, rather than a round or oval shape which Riku was used to with shinai or katanas. The grip flowered up at the top to create the hilt which hugged the base of the blade, and again at the bottom to form a diamond shaped pommel. The blade itself was silver in color but Riku had no idea what metal it was made of.

He admired the blade for a moment, which seemed almost a moment too long, before looking at an impatient Samantha in the corner of his eye. He nodded again and took a deep breath.

"Ok, here I go."

Riku made like he was going to march around the corner and face the armed guards, but suddenly he raised the sword over his head and with a loud shout split the side of the tent from top to bottom.

"There! It's open now." He smiled broadly at Samantha. She stared, wide eyed and mouth agape for a few moments before realizing what he had just done. "Go, go!" Riku urged her.

Samantha parted the tear in the tent and stumbled inside where a large gathering of dignitaries and several members of the media drank and toasted each other. They hadn't seemed to notice her yet, as her eyes darted around the room until they landed on the diamond, even more massive this close, only a few meters from where she now stood. She gasped when she saw foreign dignitaries reaching out to touch the great rock, with a sense of reverence, as they chatted and made conversation.

Unsure what to do, Samantha pushed towards the diamond in hopes that no one would recognize her as out of place. But they did, and heads began turning as she shoved

Page 88

passed one wealthy person after another while on target for her prize.

"Hey, watch it!" someone complained.

"'Scusi!" a well dressed Italian man shouted as Samantha got nearer to the diamond.

"Someone, seize that woman!" a lady with a thick British accent yelled. The scene unraveled quickly as two of the arms guards charged into the tent, guns at the ready. She was almost within reach of the diamond when she heard their voices.

"You 'tere! Put you hands ap!"

Samantha froze, her arm frozen by her side, stuck with fear. This was it, she would fail and die and the world would suffer for it.

Then there was a loud crash near the other end of the tent. Every eye turned towards the stage, where one of the large speakers had been knocked over.

"Hey everyone!" Riku shouted from the stage in very poor English. "I Godzilla! Rawr!" He swung his sword, crashing it into the riser that held the stage lights. The blade cut through the aluminum stand and brought the lights crashing down.

Samantha shook out of her frozen trance and used the diversion to reach for the diamond. She placed her right hand on it and there appeared a ghostly face floating within the rock.

"Steward," the face said, staring at her. "I see you. You will not defeat me."

In terror, Samantha almost pulled her hand away, but by sheer force of will she closed her eyes tight and focused on that feeling from before. The feeling of the Hispanic man, the feeling of the armband, the feeling she got when Aries spoke, calm and serene.

The face in the diamond screamed at fever pitch. Champagne glasses everywhere shattered, and guests covered their ears to protect from the deafening shriek. Samantha gritted her teeth and pushed harder on the diamond while Riku stopped his rampage after seeing everyone fall to the floor from the noise.

She opened her eyes just enough to see the face, now twisted with pain and anger, snapping at her hand on the other side of the diamond, as though trying to bite her.

"What…are you?" The voice inside shrieked.

"I'm The Healer. Now…heal!"

The diamond shattered. Millions of shards filled the air but didn't move, they just hung in space, each piece reverberating as the scream intensified. A million echoes from each shard echoed so that the tent itself began to shake violently. Samantha turned her eyes down to see nearly every person writhing on the floor and covering their ears was also now bleeding from the nose.

She panicked at first but a swift calm came over her. The taint was lifting.

"You want them? You have to go through me," Samantha clenched her fists and closed her eyes, focusing on the screaming voices from the shards. She felt that heat again, moving through her, around her, from her. Then one by one in quick succession the diamond shards began imploding in on themselves. And the screams died as the shards vanished into the air until at last the final piece disappeared.

When Samantha opened her eyes, Riku was next to her with a hand on her shoulder.

"We should go now. Job finished." He quickly took her by the hand and urged her along and out the way they came, while the confused crowd of guests and guards slowly began to get to their feet.

"What happened?" Samantha asked, in a stupor.

"You killed the bad guy. You did it," Riku looked over his shoulder briefly and smiled wide.

"I...did it." Samantha forced a smile, while her world began to spin, her legs gave out, and she succumbed to unconsciousness.

Chapter 8

Jude held back the tears as he stared at downtown San Francisco. The Transamerica Building looked like a great torch, with the top third of the tower consumed by roaring flames. He could faintly make out the sound of people's screams, but the fire he could hear loud and clear from his position atop the Coit Tower.

From where he stood, he could easily see the San Francisco Bay Bridge, now collapsed into the water, an effort on behalf of the National Guard in order to keep the monsters from crossing over to Oakland. The Golden Gate Bridge was also in ruins for the same reason, but it was a bit harder to see, given the smoke coming from Russian Hill, due East.

The thunderous *thwump thwump* of helicopters permeated the air, as wave after wave gathered on or near Alcatraz island. The United States military had taken up positions on the old prison for both it's proximity to and distance from the mainland. Having learned from the mistakes made in Paris, they kept their distance, yet still fired missiles into the city aimed at the Dark Ones that crawled over almost every inch like ants.

The City by The Bay was no stranger to disaster. In 1906 a deadly earthquake made parts of the city unrecognizable, and what the quake didn't destroy, the following fires did, wiping out over half of San Francisco. Then there was the Loma Prieta earthquake, dubbed the "Earthquake Series", for taking place during the 1989 World Series. With the
Page 93

expectancy of massive quakes every few decades, the government decided to tell the public this new disaster was also just an earthquake.

They even went so far as to block all non-emergency cell phone and data signals coming out of the Bay Area, to prevent the real story from getting out. But it would, eventually, reach the public when the Chaos spread to other parts of the country. And what could Jude do, standing on top of a tower gazing down at the destruction wrought by supernatural beings.

He looked down to his hands and noticed, for the first time, a pen in one hand and notebook in the other. It was odd, because he didn't remember pulling them out of his messenger bag. He flipped through the notebook to see a sketch he did of Taurus. Then another sketch of a figure he didn't recognize. He had written "Leo" under the image but it didn't ring a bell.

Jude turned his attention completely away from the terror around him to flip through page after page.

Aries.

Cancer.

Gemini "The Twins" - Taurus not a fan

Scorpio.

Jude stopped flipping through his notebook and raised his eyes again. It suddenly occurred to him that he had no memory of arriving here, in San Francisco, much less atop this tower. He slowly turned around towards the Mission District, to see hovering just above Mission Dolores, was a silhouette of a man.

He looked three dimensional, but Jude couldn't make out much more details given that the light got darker as it closed in to his person. It was almost as though he didn't emit darkness, but swallowed light.

Jude's knees buckled as he felt the same energy drain-
ing feeling he felt on top of Yggdrasil when Hat Man tried to
swallow his soul. He felt like who he was, his personality, no,
his memory was being drawn into this dark presence.

Eyes wide, his pen stabbed the notebook and he began
sketching. Then writing. Then sketching some more. He stared
at the dark man as long as his eyes would let him while his
hand flew across the page in word and art.

Sketch complete, he wrote one last word before closing
his eyes tight.

"Jude…you're dreaming. Wake up!"

Jude shot up straight under the night sky. It was clear,
there was a bright moon out, and his eyes quickly adjusted to
the dim light. He frantically searched for his notebook and
found it laying next to him in the cool green grass. He flipped
through the mostly blank pages and found none of the sketch-
es or writings from his vision. Until he came across the middle
of the notebook.

There it was, the dark image of a man, all in shadow,
no features save for the silhouette drawn in ink so hard that the
pages were indented. And beneath the image a single word
written.

"Apollyon".

"It was a vision," Taurus said, suddenly squatting next
to Jude. Jude didn't jump, even though he was a bit startled.

"I saw San Francisco. It was burning. And this guy,
Apollyon, you called him, when we were in Atlantis. He was
there. I didn't see his face though. Just this." Jude held up the
notebook. Taurus gave a long and thoughtful "hmmmmm" in
response.

Page 95

"Who is he? Who's Apollyon?"

"He is the bringer of Chaos. The Dark One through whom all Dark Ones are made. What you saw is his true form, blackness, emptiness, darkness. Though he would appear just as human as you do."

"I felt something in the dream,"

"Vision," Taurus corrected.

"I felt like my...I don't know how to describe it. My soul was being pulled out of me. But, memories too. Like if I looked too long at him, I'd even forget what he looked like. What is that?"

"Haven't you wondered already? With the history of the world and written word and records, why is there no mention of him? Or the culling? Haven't you ever wondered why great and mighty civilizations vanish without a trace and no explanation for it?" Taurus raised an eyebrow.

"You mean," Jude began as it all sunk in. "There's no record because...he made them all forget?"

"What a great trick to be able to do evil in the midst of millions and leave them all none the wiser." Taurus spat. "Mankind begins again, and again, and again, with no recollection of their mistakes, no history to learn from. So history repeats itself. We Zodiac are the shepherds of man, with the purpose of training and protecting a chosen few to keep that history alive."

Taurus hung his head and sighed heavily.

"But, if I'm the Prophet, and all I do is write stuff down, couldn't I just record everything for the next generation? The secret to computers. A secret behind Atlantis' floating city. And...and since I saw what was coming, because correct me if I'm wrong, but San Fran hasn't been destroyed yet."

Taurus nodded his confirmation.

"Then why don't I write it all down? The past, the future. Ya know," Jude waved the notebook.

"Therein lies your paradox," Taurus sat finally next to Jude.

"I don't get it."

"The Warrior has his sword. The Healer her band. The Purifier has a cistern. But The Prophet has only a pen. While you may write what was, and catalog what is, be careful of what will be. Once your pen makes that stroke, the visions you saw, are."

"Are? You mean will be?"

"No, I mean *are*. You live inside time. We exist outside it. As does Apollyon. Once you write down what you've seen of the future, it becomes a certain present."

Jude dropped the notebook and stared at Taurus. He couldn't believe his ears.

"That is the power of The Prophet. That is also your curse."

"So," Jude began, "what if I write what *could* be instead?"

Taurus smiled.

After they escaped the tent and the armed guards, Riku carried Samantha and hurried back to the shore to find Sagittarius and Aries waiting for them. Together they regrouped on the far end of the lake on the Ugandan side, well enough away that no one would have recognized them.

As Samantha regained consciousness and heaved to catch her breath, Riku paced back and forth excitedly, barely able to contain himself.

"That was amazing! Did you see that diamond shatter!? How did you do that?"

Samantha, still bent over on her knees, looked up and shook her head.

"I...have no...idea. I just...touched it." she wheezed.

"So it is done? The stone is no more?" Aries asked.

"It's done. It just...blew up and everyone...started bleeding from their...noses."

Aries reach down and touched Samantha on the back. Her breathing calmed, her heart rate normalized. She stood up straight and nodded her thanks.

"But really, I have no idea what happened. There was a face of someone or something inside the diamond. It was talking to me."

"What did it say?" Sagittarius asked.

"It called me 'steward' and say I won't defeat it," Samantha looked to Aries. "Any idea who that was?"

"It would be called, in your language, Blight." Sagittarius said, as he spat on the ground. "It is the creator of the taint, the poison that rots all things living. You stopped its poison by laying your hand on the stone. Impressive."

"Impressive? I didn't know what else to do. What was I supposed to do?"

"Heal," Aries said plainly. "All other Healers have done just that. Heal the infected. But you instead went for the source. Impressive indeed."

"Yeah, and I also helped," Riku waved his hand, feeling quite left out. "Sort of."

"If you hadn't distracted everyone, I would have been in trouble." Samantha reached out and rubbed Riku's shoulder very awkwardly. "Thanks for saving me."

Riku turned red, and unsure what to do next, bowed low.

"I was only doing my duty!" He held his posture there for an uncomfortably long time while Samantha gently backed up a few steps.

"The sword you carry, Warrior," Sagittarius' words brought Riku back to standing. "It was plunged into Yggdrasil by its last owner, the Viking I told you of. In doing this, she stopped the rotting of the great tree and turned it to stone. It was Blight that caused it to rot there."

Riku nodded then his eyes grew wide.

"She?! The Viking Warrior was a female?"

"Oh yes," answered Aries. "The stewards are never a fixed gender. We call the best fit for the position."

"Wait a minute," Samantha turned to the Zodiac. "Back in Egypt that lady said...Dr. Saliba, she said there were records of two previous stewards. A prophet and a healer."

Aries nodded.

"So this has all happened before?"

"Many times before," Aries said, "but that isn't for you to worry about. The record of the Choas is for The Prophet to manage."

"But that information is useful. If I knew how the other Healer did things that might help me now."

"Not as much as you would like," said Sagittarius. "No other Healer has succeeded like you have here. Nor Warrior where you must," he said to Riku.

"No one has ever saved the world before?" Riku asked. The two Zodiac gave each other a look.

"The world has not been threatened like it is in this age," Aries said softly.

"But you have done this before right? Saved…whoever?" Samantha pressed into Aries space.

The Timeless One lowered her head and shook it.

"No, we have never been successful in leading the stewards into victory over the Chaos."

Both Riku and Samantha gave each other a look.

"But, you will this time, yes?" Riku forced a smile.

"Each time we are called to fulfill our charge, we do so with the intent of victory," Sagittarius spoke up before Aries could answer. "This time is no different. No threat is lesser or greater than that which came before. I, we, are confident in your sure success."

No sooner did he finish his sentence than the air popped and suddenly Taurus and Jude stood among them. Riku brightened up at seeing Jude and moved to greet him.

"Prophet! You missed the battle!"

"Hey Riku…uh…Warrior. You'll have to fill me in another time." Jude patted him on the shoulder and stepped past him towards Samantha.

"You're The Healer?" Jude quickly asked her.

"Yessss. And you are?"

Jude began looking Samantha up and down, checking her arms and getting a little too close for comfort.

"Excuse me? Who are you?" she protested and pulled away.

"I'm Jude."

"The Prophet," Taurus announced from behind him. Jude rolled his eyes.

Page 100

"I'm The Prophet. If you're The Healer, shouldn't you be sick?"

"No I really shouldn't be." Samantha cocked her head. Jude turned to Taurus.

"But what I saw..."

"Changed. We changed it." Riku smiled. "We, well she, destroyed the thing that made everyone sick. We won the battle!"

Jude put his hand on his chin and began pacing.

"So I saw her get sick, and I talked about it, Riku goes to help, and it changes. Because I didn't write it down..." Jude turned to Taurus again with a smile on his face. "You were right. It does work!"

"Excuse me...what works? Why should I be sick?" Samantha was quickly losing patience.

"I see the past, no, Taurus shows me the past. I'm supposed to write down the present, but I also see the future. But not like all future just things, bits and pieces. Except recently..." Jude turned to see Aries and Sagittarius and actually looked at them for the first time.

"I've met you before, too. Well, I sketched you anyway. Aries, right?" Aries nodded. "And Sagittarius?" Sagittarius also nodded. "Leo. Where's Leo?"

"The Lion has yet to appear. He seeks The Purifier." Aries announced.

"So the order changed already. Interesting." Jude returned to his pacing.

"So if you see the future, you knew I was in trouble?" Samantha asked, Jude merely grunted a response. "So you sent Riku to help?"

"No," Riku piped up suddenly. "I wanted to help. I insisted I come to save, uh, to help you. I'm The Warrior and that's my duty."

"He did insist," Sagittarius claimed. Riku looked back at the Zodiac and received a fiery wink.

"Oh, well thank you," Samantha nodded to Riku, who in turn blushed again. "But you saw it, right?" Jude grunted his response. "So if you see the future, you know where these things are going to hit next?"

Jude stopped pacing and turned very serious. He drew near to both Riku and Samantha before speaking.

"I do. And we don't have much time if we're going to stop...him."

"Who?" Riku asked, the excitement growing on his face.

"Apollyon. He's headed to San Francisco. If we're going to stop him, we have to do it, together."

Samantha had spent three years driving around in an ambulance for a living. While most of the calls she responded to were in Queens or Brooklyn, she did on occasion have to cross into Manhattan for emergencies as well. So she was no stranger to travel, especially in traffic jams, or spending long periods of time on the road in between calls.

There were some days that were far busier than others, and although that usually meant trouble in her line of work, she enjoyed the reprieve of not having to sit in a vehicle for hours at a time. She wanted more than anything to be out helping people, not living in an oversized van, filling out paperwork and listening to the CB for incoming calls from dispatch.

So it was a massive relief for Samantha to be able to travel at the speed of light with Aries. She simply placed a golden gauntlet on Samantha's shoulder and the two appeared wherever it was they had intended to go. No traffic, no cars, no problem.

There was a slight equilibrium issue when they arrived, given that every sight, sound, and smell was suddenly very different than moments before. But Samantha was pleased to note that she had only become sick once, on the first trip around the world, and not since.

Traveling from a lake in Africa to the City By The Bay was no different for her, even though the trip was several thousand miles. It still passed by in an instant and after a few moments of catching her footing, Samantha was able to freely look around at her surroundings.

Riku, it seemed, was still adjusting to the mote of travel used by Sagittarius. He had described it a bit differently to Samantha.

"My head stretches my neck out, then my middle, then my legs. I come back together once the arrow lands though!"

Samantha felt a little sorry for him as he hunched over the neck of his horse and looked as though he might slide off onto the ground. Instinctively she reached out and touched him on the ankle and gave a thought of healing. A second later he sat up in the saddle and looked right as rain. She grinned to herself though amazingly Riku didn't seem to notice the touch.

She hadn't had much conversation with Jude yet, but he appeared behind her with the Zodiac Taurus with a popping-sound and a brush of mist. Jude was older than her by a few years, and he had a look on his face that gave off a sense of purpose, but Samantha couldn't help thinking his baby face and lack of facial hair made him look more around Riku's age. Jude began looking around immediately, and then pointed up towards Coit Tower.

"There," he said, turning to Taurus. "I was there in my dream. I could see the entire city. Can you get me up there?"

Another pop and the two vanished.

"Should we go, too?" Riku asked.

"Let us work in the shadows, Sagittarius," Aries said. He nodded his approval and moved closer to the others on his horse. Aries held her hand out towards the middle of the small circle and in the blink of an eye they were all standing, with Taurus and Jude, on top of Coit Tower.

"The observation deck is below, so we shouldn't be bothered," Jude told the others while his eyes darted around the city.

"What are we looking for?" Samantha asked.

"Ok, so over there," he pointed at the pyramid looking building, "is the Transamerica Building. That was lit like a torch. Literally. And both the Golden Gate and San Francisco Bay bridges were collapsed. But I think that was to keep the Dark Ones from crossing. And there at that old church, that's where I saw him."

"The Apollyon?" asked Riku.

"Just Apollyon. But yeah he was like, floating over the church."

"What did he look like?"

"Just a silhouette really. Just…darkness." Jude swallowed hard and continued. "Anyway, there's one problem I didn't mention."

"Which is?" Samantha crossed her arms and raised an eyebrow.

"Time. I don't exactly know when this is all going to happen. Only that it does."

"But it will happen, right?" Samantha pressured.

"Should. Should happen."

"But if it does't happen, that's good yes?" Riku spoke up, trying to share some optimism.

"Yes, and no. See it's like with you," Jude touched Samantha on the shoulder, and immediately received a glare from both her and Riku. He removed his hand.

"It's like with you. I saw you in Africa, and you were sick. But that didn't happen because Riku came to save..."

"Help..." Samantha corrected.

"Right, came to help you. So the outcome changed entirely. Us being here might be enough to stop Apollyon from showing up."

"No," Taurus said. "Look. The Chaotic One comes."

They all looked and watched as a shadow began to appear over the Mission Dolores church. There was no cloud, no object that blocked the light of the overhead sun. There was only a shadow that slowly began to darken.

"Whatever he is, we can fight him!" Riku shouted as he drew his sword.

"You have limited time before he arrives. You must decide your plan of action," Aries said to the three stewards.

"Cant you fight him?" Jude asked. "Like you did at Yggdrasil."

"Apollyon is no mere Dark One. He is darkness. We are strictly forbidden from interfering with his plan," said Taurus, "or yours." He added. Jude nodded.

"Okay then, what's our plan?"

"Evacuation," Samantha said immediately. "You all saw or heard of what happened in Paris, and Jude, you said you saw the destruction here. We have to get innocent people to safety.

"Out of the city is the only way. San Francisco has a subway system, the "Bart", I think they call it. We can get people on that. Then to the bridges. But we have to hurry."

"Sagittarius, can people see you?" asked Riku.

"No, only the stewards can see we Timeless," he answered.

"But they can see me. Get me to the train…or subway! I will get people moving."

Without another word, Sagittarius grabbed his bow, drew and loosed an arrow. Riku gave a thumbs up to his compatriots, closed his eyes tight and braced himself, then vanished.

"The people near the church will be in danger first," Samantha turned on her heels to face Jude. "How long until Apollyon gets here?"

Jude shrugged. "I honestly don't know. Minutes. Hours."

Samantha looked to Aries.

"Aries get me down as close to the mission as you can. We need to scatter people." Aries nodded and reached for Samantha but Jude interjected.

"Wait!" He quickly pulled his notebook and and closed his eyes. Without looking he jotted down a few words.

"Ok, now go." Samantha gave him a suspicious look and opened her mouth to say something, but Aries touched her shoulder and the two were gone.

"What did you write?" Taurus asked Jude.

"'Inspired by the voice and radiance of the red haired angel, the people did as she asked.'"

Taurus smiled broadly, and held both arms out to his side. The liquid gold armor surround his body once more and hardened into place. His lance materialized in his right hand, and he turned his gaze onto Jude.

"Come, Prophet. You will have need of some projection where we're headed."

Jude took Taurus' arm and the pair vanished with a pop.

Chapter 9

Somewhere out just beyond the edge of our solar system, in the coldness of space where the warmth of the sun did not reach, floated a single entity wrapped in his white robes. He watched the Earth from afar and frowned upon seeing the destruction in Paris, and the surrounding region falling into shadow. He could make out his brethren assisting the humans in their somewhat futile endeavor to save their civilization and the lives of others.

He breathed a heavy sigh.

"Beautiful, is it not?" Came a voice from behind him. "Honestly, Aquarius, I really don't know why you refuse to get a closer look."

The other man floated up beside Aquarius, the Timeless Zodiac. His robes were grey, with intricate embroidery on the hems and edges. On closer inspection one would see that the embroidery was not random at all, but rather names. The names of each and every steward, man and woman that had come before, and fallen, by his hand.

"I can see quite well enough," Aquarius said in a milder voice than his companion, "thank you very much."

"Do you ever wonder," the other man asked, placing a hand on his chin. "Do you ever wonder if they'll ever just, give up?"

"It is not in their nature to give up." Aquarius replied, crossing his arms over his chest.

"Neither was it in yours," the other teased.

"I did not give up, and you well know that."

"Of course, of course." The other became quiet for a time, also watching the events taking place on Earth.

Aquarius' eyes filled with sorrow as he watched and now listened to what was happening on top of Coit Tower. He noticed the shadow gathering on and over Mission Dolores in San Francisco. He saw the armies of Dark Ones lining up and forming ranks in what was left of Paris.

He looked away.

"Then again, I suppose I should be grateful," the other said with a smile.

"Grateful?"

"Yes. If it weren't for our agreement, I might not have enjoyed ages of sweet victory over those wretched little apes you Zodiac cling so tightly to."

Aquarius' eyes flashed. He turned to face the other and his robes blew back as though a great wind had caught them. His curly hair waved and his fists clenched.

"Now, now," the other said, "our agreement."

Aquarius took a deep breath, or made the act of doing so with no air to actually breathe in. He released his fists and returned his gaze back to Earth.

"Don't you have something to do?" Aquarius hinted at the other.

"True. I suppose I should be getting to work." The other stretched his arms wide and twisted his torso one way and then the other. He cracked his knuckles and looked over his shoulder at Aquarius.

"Don't look so grim, Aquarius. After all, they're only human." The other smiled broadly.

"You never know, Apollyon," Aquarius said without looking at him. "One day, those little apes might just surprise you."

Apollyon, the Chaotic One, The Destroyer, scoffed and turned his eyes back towards Earth. His eyes went dark, empty. He smiled at the thought of the feast to come, thousands of lives, memories, and cities would be laid to waste at his fingertips. His generals were doing their work stirring up trouble, but the real disaster was yet to come. In the darkness of his eyes he saw the Mission and a great shadow spreading over it and in the air itself. He licked his lips in anticipation.

Then he was gone, and Aquarius was alone again.

He sighed and watched with sad eyes as the three stewards had dispersed and he went to look away, but suddenly stopped. Something caught his eye so he looked closer, magnifying even the great distance at which he now saw, and read the words written on Jude's notebook.

"…the red-haired angel, the people did as she asked?' What is this, Prophet? Are you trying to…" He paused as his eyes shot wide.

"It can't be."

The next moment Aquarius was gone.

Riku landed on the steps of the subway Bart system in downtown San Francisco. Sagittarius had taken the liberty of relocating his horse to a safer area, leaving Riku for the moment alone. People gawked at him and took care to walk in a wide circle as they passed him and the sword in his hands. He lowered it and turned to shout in the loudest voice he could muster.

"Please, you have to leave! Take the train and leave the city!"

A few people gave him a look, but no one heeded his warning.

"Please, you have to leave! Danger is coming! You need to leave the city now!"

Again, no real response. Then it dawned on him. He had been talking to Samantha and Jude, and they understood him, but they were fellow stewards. Everyone here was hearing him shout, but in his native Japanese.

"Please," he tried again in his best English. "You go city or make big trouble! Oni…uh…demon come!"

This time an elderly man passed him and patted him on the back, handing him a dollar. Riku sighed, distressed, although also stuffing the dollar into his pocket. He took a deep breath and shook his head, not terribly convinced his new plan would work.

He raised the sword in front of him and charged into the subway.

"Goooodziilllla!" he screamed.

Samantha appeared a few meters in front of Mission Dolores, the oldest building in San Francisco. She thought to herself it was fitting that a being of shadow and darkness would chose this place for his grand entry. Her feet set down on a grassy median in the road, but somewhat lighter. She looked around for Aries but the Zodiac was nowhere in sight.

Samantha turned her eyes to the church as the doors opened and people began walking out.

"People, listen to me! You have to leave!" she yelled.

The group stopped cold on the steps and stared at Samantha. One elderly lady took one look and fainted. Samantha had no idea what was going on but she knew time was running short.

"Please! You are all in terrible danger! You have to leave the city, now!"

She noticed the second and third doors burst open and now a crowd was gathering from inside the church onto the steps. People looked to the sky and raised their hands, while others made the symbol of the cross over their chests and even more fell to their knees.

What is wrong with these people!? She thought.

Samantha looked up and could clearly make out the growing shadow over the church. She turned her eyes down and was shocked to see that her feet, while touching the grass, were only just. She was levitating just off the ground. She peeked over at her arms and noticed they were glowing with a golden light.

Jude! What did you write in your book?!

Samantha grit her teeth in anger, but then an idea came to her.

"I bring you a message…from…Heaven!" she announced to the gathering crowd. "The..uh..devil is coming… like he did in Paris!"

The crowd responded with gasps, oohs and ahhhs. She decided she would deal with the guilt later.

"I beg you, leave the city now. Tell your family, your friends," she held out a hand as if to touch the flock of believers. "Please, save as many as you can."

And that was all it took. The crowd quickly began to disperse, after a few snapped photos with their mobile phones, and the street filled with people heading in all directions.

Samantha almost yelped when she began to rise higher into the air.

"Well done, Healer," Aries whispered from behind her.

"Did you do all that?" Samantha whispered back.

"The glow and your angelic voice, I'm sure you couldn't hear it, was the Prophet's doing. I just played along and helped you fly."

"I'm going to kill him!" Samantha growled. Aries laughed.

Jude and Taurus appeared at the intersection of Columbus and Washington, right at the base of the Transamerica Building. Jude had to crane his neck up to see the top of the pyramid-looking tower, which had not yet been set ablaze. Cars honked at him as their drivers tried to turn down Columbus Avenue but Jude wasn't paying attention.

"Here, this is where they come from," he said to Taurus. "What's at the end of this street?"

"This road runs almost to the water itself. It ends just before Hyde Street Pier."

"That's it! They came out of the water and marched down this street and attacked this building." Jude stepped out of the street without looking at the angry drivers now laying on their horns at him. They couldn't see Taurus, they didn't have foreknowledge of the impending attack.

"The Warrior is chasing people out of the subways. The Healer was effective in evacuating the area surrounding the mission." Taurus said as he looked down the street towards the pier. "What will you do, Prophet?"

"You can't fight Apollyon, right?" asked Jude.

"Correct. We are forbidden from directly interceding against his plans."

"But you can fight the Dark Ones, like at Yggdrasil?"

Taurus looked down on the little human and smiled broadly.

"What do you have in mind?"

"Get that big spear ready."

"Lance. It's a lance." Taurus corrected. For the first time in a while Jude felt confident that maybe they had a chance. He looked up at Taurus and saw more than a Timeless, immortal being. He saw a friend.

"Apollyon isn't taking this city. We won't let him." Jude opened his notebook and began to sketch and write.

Taurus rolled his shoulders and stretched, twisting his lance in his hand.

"Here they come," the Zodiac said, with a hint of excitement in his voice.

It was dark in Paris, save for the fires that still smoldered in a few of the districts. The French government had given up trying to reclaim the city, for now, until they had a better means of fighting back against the dark invaders. Meanwhile in the darkness, hordes of Dark Ones gathered in groups, heaving and drooling as they prepared for the coming attack.

Amidst their ranks walked the living corpse, the Wicked Man. Each step he took made the sound of one thousand bones rattling, mixed with the crunching of cartilage and rotted flesh. His emaciated body kept rebuilding and regenerating itself as chunks of him would fall to the ground as he moved, effectively leaving a bloody trail of gore as he walked.

This constant reforming of his body made it appear that there were writhing snakes beneath his robes as he moved. A truly horrifying sight to behold to any except the Dark Ones that served him.

"It is time. The Master comes." He all but whispered. "Rise up Dark Ones and serve your master! The next city will now fall!"

He raised his hands up above his head and clouds began to form out of thin air. The Dark Ones snarled and gnashed their teeth and all turned their eyes upwards. The cloud grew larger and larger until it encompassed the entire area above the dark army. Then it changed in midair and rippled like water.

"Charge forward! Kill and destroy!" the Wicked Man shouted. Howls filled the air as the blanket of rippling water lowered towards the army.

"The Destroyer comes!"

One last battle cry, and the blanket of water collapsed onto the army, launching them from the streets of Paris, to the San Francisco Bay.

Samantha and Aries both looked in horror as the screaming of tourists and locals alike caught their attention. Still floating in the air above the city, they looked towards the Bay in time to see masses of black, ragged, wolf-men launching out of the waters and onto the pier.

"They have come," Aries said sullenly.

"Take me to the bridge," Samantha pointed towards the Golden Gate Bridge. "Let's see what I can do."

An otherwise tall, hulking figure crouched down on the cold dirt just outside Hammerfest, Norway. He looked across the water to the small town, the northern most town in the world, as he stalked his prey.

He was covered head to toe with golden brown furs, tied to his arms and legs with strips of leather. His hands were bare and appeared strong, but worn, as though they had seen years of hard work. His eyes were orange in color, but resembled a man's more than a cat's.

His face was covered in a thick blonde beard, with strands of white here and there that gave the impression of age. His hair was matted thick and dirty-blonde and though a bit darker than his beard, also contained white mixed in as well.

He slowly dug his fingers into the dirt and raised the mud to his nose for a smell. He nodded and grunted his approval at the scent. Today he would find his steward.

Leo the Lion, the Timeless Zodiac, charged with locating and recruiting The Purifier. Today, he would fulfill that charge.

Suddenly his eyes darted to the side as the grass nearby was disturbed by a small gust of wind. He reached for his belt and gripped the leather wrapped handle of a cudgel that hung at his side. In the next moment he sprung to life, spun round and swung the cudgel out with wide, wild eyes.

The weapon itself grew in midair, with twelve flanges on the head that encircled the piece growing outward twice their original size. Leo stopped the weapon short of demolishing his target when he recognized the face standing next to him.

"Aquarius?!" he growled.

"Good to see you too, brother," Aquarius, hands resting calmly on his robes, nodded to Leo.

"I could have killed you!" Leo laughed, putting the cudgel back on his belt as it shrunk back down to a normal size.

"I highly doubt that." Aquarius stepped forward and embraced his fellow Zodiac.

"You finally decided to come out of hiding, eh? Come to join the fight again?"

"Something to that effect," Aquarius looked out over the water and towards the town. "You seek The Purifier, yes?"

"I do," Leo rested his hands on his hips and nodded. "And I've found her. Just a matter of saying hello."

"Good. Listen to me, this is very important."

"Oh? Come to share wisdom from the stars, eh?"

"Once you have The Purifier, you must take her to the Cistern."

Leo raised his eyebrows and and lowered his arms in surprise.

"Brother, you know the Cistern has been lost to us. There's no point wasting time trying to find it. We've looked. You've looked!"

"It has not been lost. Only hidden. And I know where." Aquarius looked at Leo very seriously.

"And how do you know all this, eh? How do you know where it's hidden and we don't?"

Aquarius swallowed the lump in his throat.

"Because I'm the one who's hidden it."

Epilogue

The stage was set. The first of the twelve stewards were found, and had taken up arms against Apollyon and his dark army. Though Paris lay in ruins, the enemy had failed with their ploy in Africa. All eyes were set on San Francisco, California. The waters of the San Francisco Bay churned as Dark Ones poured out and onto the piers, attacking people and buildings alike.

Riku Yatsukura, The Warrior, wildly swung the Sword of Achilles in the underground subway in a desperate attempt to drive the populace out of danger. He heaved a heavy sigh when he noticed that, while people were running away for safety, San Francisco's finest were cautiously drawer near, pistols drawn.

Samantha Riley, The Healer, stood at the entrance to the Golden Gate Bridge and urged curious onlookers to keep moving across the bridge and away from the chaos in the water. Thanks to Jude, Samantha's countenance glowed and her voice resounded like a waterfall, giving the impression she was some sort of angelic messenger sent with a purpose. Samantha had decided to punish, and thank, Jude later for this ruse.

And Jude, The Prophet, stood behind the armor clad Zodiac Taurus, notebook in hand. He had tried once to affect the way of things with his pen and paper, using Samantha as his guinea pig, and now he'd see just how far his newfound power extended. Perhaps they could stop the Chaos here and now, before many more died.

Floating above the Mission Dolores, the great shadow had grown and now suddenly collapsed on itself. It consolidated and shook the very air around it. Peels of thunder shot out and resonated through nearby neighborhoods in sharp succession, giving them an almost eerie rhythm.

Like that of laughter.

The shadow twisted and warped and began to take on the appearance and shape of a man, clothed in dark robes.

"Cry…and…despair," came a cackling voice from the void. "I, The Destroyer, Apollyon, have come!"

To Be Continued in

The Timeless Zodiac
Book II

Jude Schreiber

Birthday: May 1
Zodiac Sign: Taurus
Location: California, USA
Height: 180cm
Occupation: Tech support
Likes: Dungeons & Dragons
Dislikes: Responsibility

Taurus

Weapon: The Tome

A notebook, though the true weapon lays in the words written within.

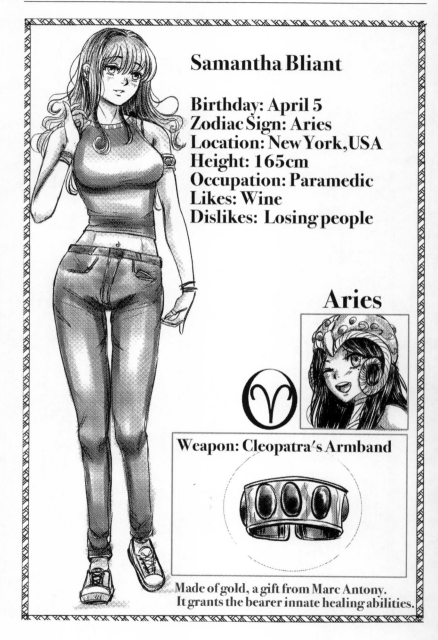

Samantha Bliant

Birthday: April 5
Zodiac Sign: Aries
Location: New York, USA
Height: 165cm
Occupation: Paramedic
Likes: Wine
Dislikes: Losing people

Aries

Weapon: Cleopatra's Armband

Made of gold, a gift from Marc Antony.
It grants the bearer innate healing abilities.

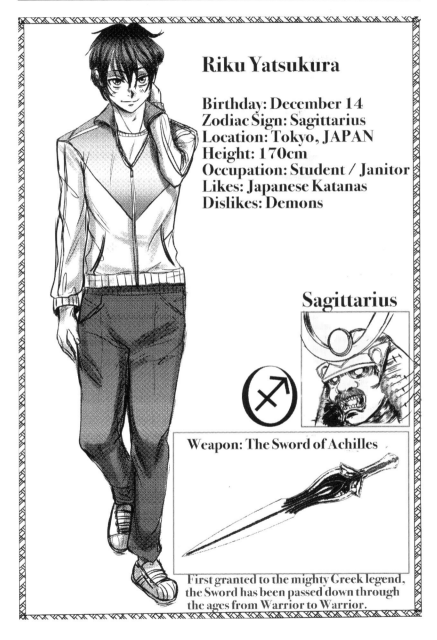

Riku Yatsukura

Birthday: December 14
Zodiac Sign: Sagittarius
Location: Tokyo, JAPAN
Height: 170cm
Occupation: Student / Janitor
Likes: Japanese Katanas
Dislikes: Demons

Sagittarius

Weapon: The Sword of Achilles

First granted to the mighty Greek legend,
the Sword has been passed down through
the ages from Warrior to Warrior.

68246360R00081

Made in the USA
Columbia, SC
06 August 2019